# After the Famine

Colette McCormack

**ATTIC PRESS**
Dublin

First published in 1996 by
Attic Press
29 Upper Mount Street
Dublin 2

A Catalogue record for this title is available from the British Library.

ISBN 1 85594 142 2

Cover Illustration: Angela Clarke
Origination: Attic Press
Printing: The Guernsey Press Co. Ltd

# After the Famine

# About the Author

Colette McCormack is a writer and bookseller who contributes a regular column to *Books Ireland*. She is the author of the bestselling *Mary-Anne's Famine*. She lives in County Kildare.

# Dedication

To Brian O'Reilly and the boys of Sixth Class (1995), Our Lady of Victories Boys' National School, Ballymun Road, whose 150th Famine Commemoration Exhibition I was proud to view.

To all the girls and boys who sent me their book reviews of *Mary-Anne's Famine* and their Famine Poetry.

To Joan and Henry McDowell in appreciation of their help and encouragement.

To Ber and Marty in Florida with love.

# Glossary

| | |
|---|---|
| *Risteárd na Crann* | Richard of the Wood |
| *a mhic* | my son |
| *a ghrá* | my love |
| *Fraoch Bán* | white heather |
| *céilí* | a dance/gathering of Irish people |
| *alanna* | my child, term of endearment |
| *Sasannach* | Englishman |
| *Lá Ceoil* | Day of Music |
| *fleadh* | festival |
| *sean-nos singer* | singer of unaccompanied Irish songs |
| *Lá Ceoil agus Taispeantais Ceardaíochta* | Day of Music and Craft Display |
| *Éire beo, Éire go deo* | Ireland alive, Ireland for ever |
| *sos beag* | short rest |
| *arís* | again or repeat |
| *as Gaeilge* | speaking in Irish |
| *sheancaí* | story teller |
| *scéal* | story |
| *dúidín* | clay pipe |
| *cáibín* | cap |
| *prátaí* | potatoes |
| *a stóir* | sweetheart or darling |
| *Is tú grá mo chrói, Máire Aine* | It is you who are the love of my heart, Mary-Anne |
| *póirín* | small potatoes |
| *clochán* | old stone structure |
| *crios/criosanna* | belt/s |
| *sugán stools* | stools with seats woven from dried rushes |

# Prologue

*I want you to know who I am, where I come from and how I live in this time, so you will always remember and pray for me ....*

Thus begins the story of Mary-Anne Joyce, who lived in the small village of Moneen in County Galway, in the middle of the last century, and who kept a journal of the events of her life during the Famine.

It was the year 1845 and the potato crop had been ruined by a mysterious disease which had overnight turned the healthy green potato plants into a black evil smelling mess. The people of Moneen, in common with the majority of Irish people at that time, depended solely on the potato for their staple diet. The failure of the crop was a calamity of country wide proportions and thousands of men, women and children slowly starved to death. Wheat, oats, barley and meat were exported from Ireland at the behest of the Government at the time. The country was over flowing with good food but the people of Ireland were denied access to it. Thousands who were able to do so, emigrated to the new worlds of America and Canada. Many died on the 'coffin ships' during the long weeks of travel in terrible conditions.

Mary-Anne, her mam and dad and Mamo Cait struggled to survive the year of 1845 by eating nettles, fruit and berries and by grubbing around in the fields for whatever could be gathered from the ruined potato crop. Póiríns, which would have normally been fed to the pigs, were gratefully collected and eaten.

There were hopes that the potato crop of 1846 would be alright, but in June of 1846 the disease struck again. The fear and terror of the people was terrible to behold. There was nothing ahead for them but a slow painful death. Their last hope was gone.

The Joyce family had to leave their home and country to survive, and we read of the sorrow and the sadness of emigration which they endured. Mary-Anne has continued to keep a journal of the happenings of the time and of her new life in New York. She intends to return to live in Ireland sometime, and keeps this thought firmly in her mind as she begins her new life in America.

# One

Tim O'Connor rocked back and forth on his heels to keep his circulation going as he stood on duty at the corner of Wyndham and Gramercy, awaiting the arrival of his relief man. There was a sharpish breeze whistling around the corner. Tim's mind was active with thoughts other than about his police work. His evening study classes were keeping him occupied and with the prospect of final examinations being held in another few weeks he was working late into the nights on his books, consequently he was tired and not up to his usual good form. As well as his studies he had several other problems on his mind, not the least of which was a letter he had received from home giving news of his father's failing health. Mary-Anne Joyce, his 'little Irish sweetheart' as he labelled her in his own mind, was another of his 'problems' as was Miss Janine Wiseman.

Tim was baffled as to why Miss Janine should be on his mind at all. He had met her at her birthday ball some weeks back, at what had been a great and exciting evening for him. He had been observing for years the lifestyle of the wealthy people living in the section of New York city which he patrolled when on duty. That he would ever cross the threshold of one of those fine houses had not even been considered by him, but now, through knowing Mary-Anne, he had not only crossed the threshold but had been introduced to and had waltzed with the daughter of

11

one of their owners. This was one of the aspects of American life which appealed to him. The class distinction at home in Ireland - a penny looking down on a ha'penny - would never have allowed for a similar happening. However, thank God, America was a young country where every person was deemed equal, and where you could have a chance of succeeding in whatever ambition you might aspire to. Hard work paid off, not like at home where you could work your fingers to the bone for your landlord and master, and be no better off for that.

Janine Wiseman was the only daughter of well-to-do parents who indulged her every whim. Her delicate constitution and their wealth allowed them to cosset and pamper her. She was not unaffected by this care and attention, but for all that, she had never known hardship, she remained a kind and loving girl. Tim recalled how much he had enjoyed dancing with her and how easy it was to talk with her. Giving himself a mental shake to recall him to the real world of peacekeeping, he decided to walk further up the avenue on the look-out for his relief man who was by now at least ten minutes late for the change-over. However his mind drifted away again and he thought about his own family, the O'Connors of Kerry. All right, so there was a big difference between Tim O' Connor of present day New York and Janine Wiseman of Gramercy Avenue, but the O'Connor clan, a proud and ancient family were direct descendants of the O'Connor Don, who was himself a direct descendant of Turlough O'Connor, the last High King of Ireland. Tim had been reared with the pride of this ancient clan and he knew all the history which was available about them.

Turlough was a powerful ruler and a very learned man. He had churches built and because of this students from the continent kept returning to Ireland to study at Clonmacnoise, Armagh and Lismore. The island of saints and scholars was once again providing education and culture for its own people and those from other countries.

The O'Connors came to County Kerry in a circuitous fashion. During the reigns of Queen Mary and Queen Elizabeth, the O'Connors, who were then in Leix and Offaly, were driven off their lands and went across country, first to Cong in County Mayo, and then on to Roscommon. There they built an abbey in Ballintubber, which alas, was demolished during the period of the Penal Laws. The O'Connor clan then went to County Clare, and thence, at a later date, they crossed into County Kerry. There they occupied Carrigafoyle Castle on the banks of the Shannon. Once more they were driven from their chosen site, this time by Earl Fitzmaurice, who himself owned most of the land in North Kerry. Eventually they settled in the Glenbeigh area of West Kerry. The most well known of Tim's antecedents who settled in the Glenbeigh area was Risteárd na Crann, so called because he worked at tree planting.

All of his life Tim had been familiar with his ancient lineage and the pride of the O'Connor clan was very much a part of his make-up. He often mused on the historical past of his family and determined that at some future date he would make a life for himself again in Glenbeigh. When he considered how his parents were struggling to eke out a meagre living on their small holding, they who were the direct descendants of the High King of Ireland, he had made a promise to himself. He swore that one day, by his own efforts or those of future family, the O'Connor land would be returned to the O'Connor clan.

\* \* \* \* \*

Tim was awakened from his reverie by a slap on the back and a cheerful voice beside him saying 'Tim, me oul' pal, you surely are miles away'. Thomas Hayden, a Kildare man, gave him a slight push. 'Wake up there man, time you were goin' back to sign off.'

Tim forbore from reminding him that he, Thomas, was nearly fifteen minutes late in letting him off duty, and enquired 'Tell me, Thomas, how are things at home with your family? Do you hear from them often?'

'As you probably know, Tim, a mhic, Kildare has so far escaped the worst of the hunger, but food is now gettin' scarce, the weather is fierce bad, and the crops are waterlogged in the ground,' Thomas answered. 'To tell the truth I'm awful lazy about sending letters home. My mam writes regular enough, God bless her, and I am ashamed at the long delays before I do answer her letters. 'Tis a lazy divil I am, no doubt about it,' he spread out his hands resignedly, 'but that's how it goes.'

'You should try to keep in touch with home, Thomas, they love getting letters from over here, you know,' Tim said. 'Anyway, I must be off, I'll see you tomorrow.' Tim nodded to Thomas and moved away towards the precinct, turning up the collar of his tunic against the cool breeze.

Thomas Hayden watched Tim as he went along the street and then took up his position. He felt somewhat guilty having been reminded by the conversation with his comrade of his own tardiness in writing home to his family. 'Come a day, go a day, God send Sunday, that just about describes me,' he thought, 'I'll just have to pull my socks up and put pen to paper. I'll do it this evening when I come off duty.' That decision made he adjusted his helmet, tightened the strap of his truncheon firmly around his wrist and stepped off on his tour of duty up the Avenue.

Meanwhile Tim reached the precinct, signed himself off duty and made his way to the dayroom to leave in his equipment. He took the letter from home from his jacket pocket and read it again. His mother wrote that the cabin roof was leaking and needed re-roofing badly, the stock was in poor condition, his father no longer in the best of health. Money was needed for so many things, not the least of which was food. His younger brothers worked hard and long, but it was a case of one step forward and two steps backwards in Ireland at the present time, and for the foreseeable future. The money he sent home was most welcome. 'God Bless you son, and come home soon', she wrote and signed it as always, 'Your loving Mother.'

Tim recalled the farewells at the docks when the common saying was 'Goodbye, God bless and send home the slates'. Many a poor emigrant kept this in mind and sent home whatever could be afforded towards the re-roofing of the cabin, and here was his own poor mother driven to asking for the same. A proud woman, she had always encouraged her son to do as well as he could 'over there' and if he could see his way to returning home in five years or less, the promise of this would be a great comfort to her. Neither his father nor herself demanded too much from him, and things must be very bad when she had to mention the condition of the roof.

Tim squeezed his eyes tightly closed to keep the tears from falling. He folded the sheet of paper and tucked it carefully into his pocket.

# Two

Mary-Anne passed the smoothing iron over the silken garment on the work table. Her mind was busy in time with her hands as she ironed, folded and put aside each item of clothing belonging to her young mistress, Miss Janine Wiseman. This was a daily chore for Mary-Anne but she enjoyed caring for the beautiful clothing of her charge and always treated the fragile lace, silks, and other delicate materials with great care and attention. Her mind wandered off in varying directions as she automatically carried out the work. She was thinking this morning of something which she had read in the newspaper, which was passed down to the kitchen each day when the family upstairs had finished perusing it. In the section 'Irish news at Home and Abroad' it was stated that a 'well-known Young Irelander would be holding a meeting in the Fraoch Bán drinking emporium on East 86th Street, on Tuesday, June 11th, 'to raise funds for the starving people in far off Ireland'. Mary-Anne knew this man to be a revolutionary in the main, but was attracted to the meeting herself by the fact that 'fund-raising' was to be the theme of the evening. She had never forgotten about the people at home, although she was living nigh on four years in the United States, so she always tried to contribute something, however small, to any collections made for the purpose of helping the destitute. As she waited for the heavy smoothing iron to cool a little she planned how she would encourage her family and friends to go along to the meeting and contribute as best they could.

There was a strong group of people in New York who sought donations through priests and small shop-owners. These people insisted that no decent Irish man or woman could refuse to give something, however small. Mary-Anne always gladly gave her few cents whenever she got an opportunity to do so. Not so Tim O'Connor, she smiled to herself as she remembered ... he was inclined to mutter under his breath about the improbability of the main sum reaching the troubled people for whom it was intended. The Young Irelanders who had reached the safety of America were loud in their cries for revenge on those who had caused the part destruction of the Irish nation. People, many of them struggling to live in the new homeland, dug deep into their pockets in their misguided belief that the bulk of the collections would reach the famished people at home in Ireland.

'Tim, you are a doubting Thomas,' she often chided him, seeing his reluctance when faced with a collection bowl. 'Of course these people are downright honest, they are doing this for charity as you well know.'

'I have a feelin' about this crowd,' Tim defended himself, 'and these feelin's that I do have are nearly always right.'

'Oh go on, Tim, why would anybody want to cheat like that,' Mary-Anne had teased him. 'Anyway, why don't you organise something yourself to raise funds?'

'Bedad and you have something there, Mary-Anne,'

Tim had exclaimed. 'A great idea, just leave it with me and I will come up with a fine way of raising money, besides shoving a bowl under people's noses.' The two of them had laughed at the mere idea, but knowing Tim as she now did Mary-Anne believed that he would find a way.

Mary-Anne tidied away the work table and put Miss Janine's garments neatly in her bureau. Her afternoon was free as Miss Janine was visiting with her grandmother. She had an appointment with Tim as he also was free of evening duty this week. As it was a nice sunny day Mary-Anne decided to wear a cotton dress with a lightweight pelisse over it and she would wear her blue bonnet to match her dress. She hastened to ready herself as Tim was never late and she preferred to be punctual herself.

Tim, as usual, called to the downstairs door for her and the two of them set off on yet another tour of the fine city of New York. Today they planned to visit the area known as the garment section, where the infamous sewing factories abounded. As they strolled the narrow streets lined with tall buildings they observed the barred windows, and both began to feel thoroughly uncomfortable and annoyed when they considered the many women who were virtually locked into these places until the whistle blew to denote closing time.

'Honest to God, Mary-Anne,' Tim exclaimed, 'I do be having nightmares about these places. Can you imagine what it would be like if a fire broke out in one of them?' He gestured towards the gaunt grey buildings wherein the unfortunates had to earn their living in desperate conditions. Mary-Anne shivered at the thought of such a calamity.

'Oh, Tim, don't you be saying things like that, we'll have to find a different direction to walk next week, so you'll have no more nightmares. '

Tim had to laugh. 'Ah, you are right, Mary-Anne, don't you be minding me, I have a great imagination, you know. But, you and I have to get to know this great city, every inch of it, and when we have all that done, then we will go across the river and have a look at New Jersey.'

He took her hand and began to run, Mary-Anne held onto her bonnet and tried to keep up with him, pleading with him to slow down. It was a beautiful clear day in early summer, the best time of the year in New York, before the dreaded heat of July and August. The two of them stopped, laughing and breathless at the steps to the cathedral. 'Come on in and we'll say a prayer,' Tim suggested, 'we'll say a prayer that we'll come up with a good plan for raising money for Ireland.'

Mary-Anne and Tim climbed the steps and went in through the wide open door into the dimly lit church. The smell of incense and candle wax wafted around them. They found that they were whispering and walking on tiptoe as they made their way up the long aisle towards the main altar. There were other people kneeling throughout the vast building and the atmosphere was calm and peaceful. Mary-Anne whispered to Tim that she was going to look for Our Lady's altar to say a few Hail Marys, and he whispered back to go ahead and he would look around the church.

Tim studied the splendid stained glass windows,

the vaulted roof and the wooden depictions of the Way of the Cross. This great church was a far cry indeed from the simple country church in Glenbeigh where he had been baptised and received the Sacraments. In fact his local parish church of the Good Shepherd in Manhattan was a very ordinary church in comparison. He touched the letter in his pocket remembering its contents and in that moment a feeling of utter loneliness and sadness came over him. He had not felt this way in a long time, but now he wanted to see his mother and father, to touch them, to embrace them, to tell them that he loved them. He had to hold on tightly to the wooden rail in front of him to stop himself from running down the aisle in a panic to reach home. Three thousand miles separated him from his family, three thousand long unattainable miles.

When Mary-Anne turned and came back down the aisle towards Tim, she realised immediately that he was deeply upset.

'Tim, whatever is the matter?' She touched his arm gently.

Tim relaxed his grip a little and looked down at her anxious face, he was trembling and on the verge of tears.

'Mary-Anne, such a longing for home came over me just now, I just can't think straight at the minute. I was sure that I was well settled here, but I am not, I want to go home.'

Mary-Anne could feel the tears well up in her own eyes and she placed her two hands on his shoulders, 'Oh, Tim, please don't, it's a perfectly natural feeling to have. I do be terrible sad sometimes myself and me with my mam and dad here.'

'As you know, Mary-Anne, most of the time I do be in good form, coddin' and goin' on, you see it keeps me from thinkin' too deep,' Tim tried to explain, 'but sometimes I do be nearly overcome by the desperate loneliness.'

The two of them walked out of the church and stood on the steps looking down at the wagons, the coaches and the people passing down below.

'I'll never get used to this place, I am going to have to do somethin' about getting money together to go home to Kerry,' Tim stated. 'Maybe I'll look for work on the railroads'.

Mary-Anne was really shocked 'Tim, you wouldn't work on the railroads, there are dreadful things happening all the time. I do hear Mam and Dad talk about what goes on, the terrible accidents, the fights, you would not like that type of work at all. Come along, we will call to see Frau Gruber, you will feel better when you have something to eat. Mam always says that people feel better when their stomachs are good and full.'

'Poor Mary-Anne and you on your day off, having to listen to me and my complainin'' Tim gave a little laugh. 'I'm sorry, a ghrá, it was the letter from home that set me off,' he put his arm around her shoulder and gave her a quick hug, 'you're right, we will go to the tea rooms, it's a bit of a walk from here, so off we go.' There was a smile back on his lips and his eyes were regaining their customary gleam; Tim O'Connor was coming back from the edge of loneliness.

# Three

That night Mary-Anne sat cross-legged on her bed writing about the happenings of her life in New York, a little job she never ever forgot to do each day. No matter what else might need to be done she always found time to note down each day's events. She was still worried about Tim O'Connor and the desperation which had caused him to lose his composure in the cathedral earlier that day. On their way to Frau Gruber's establishment she had tried to comfort him and assure him that there was nothing shameful about being lonely for his parents and his home. Most of the Irish living around them most likely felt exactly the same as he. She herself had developed a patience about her own particular need to return to Ireland. She knew that she would go back home one day, so for the time being she was able to go about her life in as calm a way as possible.

She was enjoying her time working for the Wiseman family and was able to save a little money from her wages; this she kept hidden in a shoe box beneath her bed. Every now and again she would take out the box, shake the money out onto the bed and lovingly count it. It was her secret 'home to Galway' money and she always felt comforted and content as it slowly increased towards sufficient for a one way ticket to Ireland.

The family were very kind and good to Mary-Anne, and to their staff in general. They themselves had come to America from Poland, with no more than the clothes on their backs, as Miss Janine had informed her, and by plenty of studying and working at whatever they could, had gradually established themselves in the life of the city of New York. They never forgot their roots, they never forgot their own hard times, and Mary-Anne realised quite early on in their employ that she was a very lucky girl to have secured her position with them.

\* \* \* \*

Following the excitement of the party for Miss Janine's eighteenth birthday, life had resumed an even pace in the house on Gramercy Avenue. Miss Janine's health was improving all the time and she was able to go out and about again. They had resumed their outdoor trips in the dog-cart with Beauty back between the shafts again, and the glorious weather made New York look splendid, the green buds showing on the trees and the spring flowers moving in the gentle breeze. Miss Janine was having her portrait painted which involved sittings for two or more hours at a time. Mary-Anne, therefore, had more free time than she would normally have, and was spending this creating her own story for younger children - another jealously guarded secret. She was finding it a delight to note down the story, her imagination in full flight, and as the pages filled she realised that here was her true vocation. With the help of her friend Seán Thornton and the permission given by Dr Wiseman to use the facilities of his library her command of the English language had improved steadily. She intended to let Seán read the first few chapters when she had progressed that far, as he had always encouraged her to write, and she knew that he would give his true opinion of her work.

It was intended, since Miss Janine's health was maintaining a steady progress, that she would now be ready to take riding lessons, and in the coming weeks a suitable pony would be selected and stabled at the rear of the house along with the carriage horses and Beauty. Lessons would commence within a short time. There was also talk of a trip to Europe. Mary-Anne did not in the least envy her charge these extras in her life. That was the way the better-off people lived, and that was accepted, and she herself was very fortunate that life was so good for her and for her family in this great city of New York. Her parents plans for moving to their newly-acquired small holding in the Catskill area of the state were progressing well and though they had suggested on several occasions that Mary-Anne might consider moving up there with them they did not put her under any undue pressure to do so. She was quite well satisfied with her life at the present time.

\* \* \* \*

Seán Thornton continued to work as tutor to Miss Janine for three days a week. He found that she was quite proficient in her studies with the exception of the French language. Her understanding of the language was a rather slow process, and on occasion Seán had begun to wonder if she was making a genuine effort to attain even a basic knowledge. However, he did not wish to discommode the young lady by remarking on her laxity in this area while she was way ahead in the other subjects. Unknown to him Miss Janine had confided to Mary-Anne that she was deliberately being obtuse regarding the foreign language being taught to her, as she hoped to prolong Seán's stay as her tutor for as long as possible.

It was quite evident to Mary-Anne that Seán Thornton occupied a great deal of her young charge's thoughts. She was often in a pensive mood after morning lessons, and liked to question Mary-Anne on Seán's life while he lived in Ireland, and also how he occupied his time in New York after the daily lessons in Gramercy Avenue. In truth Mary-Anne could not give her any information about how Master Thornton spent his free time. She knew that he had taken a room a distance away from her parents in Coburg Street, but she had no knowledge of how his spare time was spent.

They met on occasion in the environs of the house in Gramercy and would speak together whenever the opportunity arose. There was a special closeness between them following on from the birthday party when they had danced together and Seán had called her 'mavourneen', the old Irish pet name. Mary-Anne had spent many an evening lying in her bed going over and over the waltz she had had with Seán, and many a cozy time was spent cuddled in her warm bed weaving fanciful dreams about life in which both Seán Thornton and Tim O'Connor figured largely. These were 'comfort day-dreams' and very pleasant to indulge in before falling asleep each night.

Mary-Anne decided to approach Seán when the occasion arose to ask him if he would be at all interested in going to the fund raising evening in the Fraoch Bán on the llth of the month. She had never been to an evening devoted to this cause. Her father and mother were prepared to support any collections being made for the poor at home, but were not anxious to go to any fund-raising affairs. They considered that to become involved in this way could possibly lead to involvement of a more militant kind which they could not condone.

Mary-Anne got her opportunity to speak with Seán Thornton earlier than expected. She had just finished pegging some garments out to dry in the kitchen garden when she spied Seán returning from his usual morning stroll, a short break from his lessons with Miss Janine.

'Good morning, Mary-Anne, and how are you today,' he greeted her cheerfully.

'I'm grand, thanks,' she replied. 'I'm glad I have met you, Seán. I was wondering would you be interested in coming to a fund-raising evening on Tuesday in a place called the Fraoch Bán on East 86th Street?' She glanced enquiringly at him when he began to laugh. 'Would you believe it, Mary-Anne, but I was about to ask you the same thing myself.' Mary-Anne joined in his laughter at the coincidence.

'I don't know if they look kindly on ladies entering these establishments,' Seán remarked, 'but you'd be interested in going?'

'Well, yes I would, seeing as it is for the people at home,' Mary-Anne answered.

'We'd like to think that that is where it would be

going all right,' Seán said.

Mary-Anne thought to herself that Tim O'Connor was not alone in his doubting apparently, and asked 'Do you have some doubts about where the money will be going, Seán ?'

'All I will say on that score,' Seán stated 'is that I hope the money goes to the cause to which people have subscribed.' And no more would he say on the matter.

The Irish-American newspapers which her dad got regularly, often complained that Irish emigrants were not prepared to integrate into the society of their adopted land. No, they preferred to live together, generally in unacceptable areas, were not inclined towards cleanliness, and carried on with their wakes, weddings and frolics as they had at home. This meant that they did not get any opportunity to observe the American way of life. In actual fact, Seán Thornton himself maintained during one of his discussions with Mary-Anne on this subject, that many of the Irish people *had* come into contact on *many* occasions with native American prejudice and retreated back into their own ghettos for mutual protection, preferring their own way of life to this new unacceptable one. When faced with signs 'No Irish need apply' posted up on factories and building sites it was natural that one would retreat to the comfort of one's own people.

There was also a very high mortality rate in the grossly overcrowded and unsanitary housing conditions. Some people lived in cellars which were very often flooded with rainwater and raw sewage. Others lived in shanty huts, made out of rough wood, and in the depths of winter - and winter in New York was far more severe than that which Irish people had known - people had on occasion frozen to death. John Hughes, the Bishop of New York maintained that the Irish very often had left horrific living conditions in Ireland to live in even worse places in their newly adopted country. These conditions very often led to crime, violence, drunkenness and insanity.

Mary-Anne was familiar with the stories of unfortunates who had left home with great hopes of a new life and found themselves in such dire circumstances that they were unable to even hope to scrape their way out. Her mam and dad, had, in their charity gone around with members of their local parish church to try to relieve the want of these unfortunates. The bishops and priests believed that alcohol was the downfall of many of the Irish immigrants, the change in the weather, lack of familiar food and clothing, and the psychological difficulties resulting from unfamiliar situations, causing people to drink to excess to try to forget their problems. Unfortunately, all this carry on, which included fist fighting, public violence and crime, was all too prevalent amongst the Irish. Those of the Irish who tried to live a decent life, and rear their families to the best of their abilities, found themselves lumped together with their intemperate countrymen, and this caused them intense feelings of aggravation.

As Mary-Anne walked alongside Seán her mind was occupied with these thoughts and Seán was silent also, only occasionally reminding her to take care of her dainty boots on the rough surface of the streets. 'Your boots that you wore at home in Galway would be well suited to these rough and stony ways,' he remarked on one occasion when they were negotiating a particularly unkempt stretch of roadway. Mary-Anne had to agree with him. The shoes which she wore were a pair which Miss Janine had complained were too tight for her and had passed on to Mary-Anne. They were made of fine calfskin and high buttoned and suited Mary-Anne's outfit, specially worn for the outing with Seán. They were delicately made and designed for smooth pathways and certainly not for the rough and stony streets of the city. Nevertheless, Mary-Anne was very proud of them and pleased that Seán had actually noticed their fineness and soft texture.

They reached the emporium and Seán guided her inside the main entrance. There was a goodly number of people standing around the inner doors. Some were eminently respectable looking, some were obviously 'shanty town' people, and the language being spoken by all was the Irish language. As Mary-Anne listened to the soft 'hiss' of conversation, she felt a great kinship with the people there. She had been speaking English now for a few years and it was only when she went home to visit with her family that she got the opportunity to speak 'as Gaeilge'. Seán and Tim both, on occasion, would lapse into their native tongue when speaking with her or together, but for the most part she spoke in English in her place of employment. She realised, of course, that to make one's way in a strange country one must learn the language of that country. She knew many an Irish immigrant who would not or could not speak any language other than Irish.

The interior of the emporium was dimly lit but it was obvious that men made up the bulk of the audience, although there were two or three other girls there as far as Mary-Anne could discern. The crowd was ushered through the foyer and into a room opening on the right hand side. As they took their seats Mary-Anne glanced around on the chance that she might recognise any of the people present. When everyone was finally seated a door at the rear of the room opened and two men entered and took their places at a raised platform at the top of the room.

Seán nudged Mary-Anne and whispered, 'See that man on the right up there? He is Dick O'Connell, one of the Young Irelanders who managed to get safely over here, and the other one is James Morgan, both strongly nationalistic, and very anti-British.'

'How do you recognise them, Seán' Mary-Anne asked. Seán hesitated a little before he answered ....

'To tell you the truth, Mary-Anne, this is not the first of this type of meeting that I have attended.' Mary-Anne looked at him in amazement ....

'Goodness, Seán, I didn't know that, you mean you have been at fund-raising evenings already? That is great to hear.'

'Raising funds is only part of what this particular group do,' Seán replied. 'I cannot tell you more than that at this time'. Mary-Anne was by now really intrigued. Seán Thornton was once again surprising her - an unknown quantity this friend of hers.

Seán continued to converse with her as there was some debate going on between the two men at the top table. 'You recall the failure of the rising of the Young Irelanders last year, Mary-Anne, in which I took part?'

Mary-Anne nodded.

'It is very difficult to raise money for arms, so if it is said that any money raised at these functions will go towards the purchase of food, then people will contribute. You see, before the Rising, so I am reliably informed, enthusiasm was high in America, and the Irish in this country and those of first generation families, held monster rallies, raised money, purchased arms and had armed men on the ready for overseas service should they be needed. Do you know, Mary-Anne, that even the Bishop of New York, His Lordship John Hughes, who is from the County Tyrone, helped with money himself and urged his parishioners to do likewise. Following the defeat in Tipperary however, many people withdrew in shame, others argued over how the remaining funds would be used. The priests at home were not too pleased by this and through their influence, many of the more affluent Irish Americans withdrew their support from these revolutionaries and things haven't been too good for them since.' Seán finished his conversation when the two men faced their audience and gave instructions for the meeting to begin.

It was an orderly and well conducted meeting. However, it was obvious that hatred for all things English was the main thread running through the proceedings. One man who spoke from the floor claimed that his one wish was that his children would return to Ireland and that they would carry rifles and arms to clear the enemy from the country. Another man claimed that the Famine was God venting his anger for the sins of many, and that he himself suffered greatly from shame that he had fled the country during its most tragic time. He would return one day to fight for the rights of the people who had remained behind, and in this way he might free himself of the guilt which was destroying him. 'I drink more than I should,' he finished, 'because I can not live with these feelings. I deserted Ireland.'

One of the men at the top table rose and spoke. His voice was harsh and it was obvious that he was very angry. 'Remember, remember, all you at this meeting, that we were driven out of Ireland by cruel exercise of power; we were forced to accept ignominy and humiliation beyond man's endurance. I say to you remember these things all your lifetime, and make sure your children know of them too.' Loud applause greeted these pronouncements. Then another speaker praised the 'great country we live in, good money can be earned on the railroads and there is food-a-plenty for all'.

Then to Mary-Anne's amazement Seán Thornton rose and requested permission to speak. 'Gentlemen and ladies present, this meeting was called for the purpose of fund-raising to feed the starving people at home. I have yet to hear one word regarding this. Money will do more good for those poor folk than all the cries for vengeance that I hear in this room. Thank you.' He took his seat.

There was absolute silence for a time in the room. The audience turned to observe this man who had the temerity to challenge the leaders at the top table.

'Your name, sir?' The man Mary-Anne knew now as Dick O'Connor rose and banged the table with his fist. 'Your name and credentials this instant,' he

33

demanded. By now Mary-Anne was shaking with nervousness, and she clasped her hands together with fear.

Seán rose again.

'I am Seán Thornton, formerly schoolmaster in Ireland, now living in this country to earn my living.' Seán's voice was calm and controlled.

'So you think you know better than the rest of us, do you?' The other man spoke harshly. 'You wouldn't have known much about hunger in your position in life and you are refusing to recognise the real causes of the hunger in Ireland. What kind of an Irishman are you, anyway?' He leaned towards Seán.

'I know the facts the same as yourself, sir,' Seán replied quietly, 'but people are starving, dying indeed as I now speak, dying in ditches at home in Ireland, suffering from terrible diseases. Money is what is needed for their relief, they cannot eat words so I say, less talking of what cannot be rectified presently, and more planning and effort to raise money to try to alleviate some of the want.'

To Mary-Anne's surprise there were encouraging comments from around the room, and she reached for Seán's hand when he regained his seat, and his fingers tightened over hers. 'The quiet man' had once again confounded her and her admiration for him was total. He was not entirely unmoved by the stand he had taken, as she could detect a slight tremor in his fingers as she held his hand.

'You were very brave, Seán,' she whispered.

'Not a bit of it, Mary-Anne,' he whispered back, 'but it had to be said, I have been to similar meetings before, and so much time and energy was wasted going back over old wrongs.'

The meeting continued with discussions on the ways and means of raising money. It was agreed on church collections, rallies, céilís in parish halls, door to door appeals, and card-playing in groups, so much to be charged for each person taking part. Names were taken of those willing to help and both Mary-Anne and Seán added their names to the list sent around the room for this purpose. The meeting ended with arrangements for a further gathering in a week's time, when details of the fund-raising efforts would be finalised. Time was vital and the sooner money could be collected and on its way to Ireland the better.

Dick O'Connor then rose and in a powerful baritone voice sang:

*O Father dear the day will come when vengeance loud will call,*
*And we will rise with Erin's boys to rally one and all*
*I'll be the man to lead the van beneath our flag of green,*
*and loud and high will raise the cry 'Revenge for Skibbereen.*

The assembled crowd joined in with him and at the words 'Revenge for Skibbereen', boots were pounded on the wooden floor and fists punched the air. The mood of the crowd was jovial, but Mary-Anne noticed that the two men whom Seán had challenged were observing him with cold eyes and closed faces. Those men do not like Seán, she thought with fear in her heart.

As they left the meeting hall, one of the attendance approached them and offered his hand.

'You said the right thing in there, Seán Thornton,' he said, 'a lot of good time is spent carelessly at meetings like that one. I'm glad to make your acquaintance, I'm from the county Wexford, Pat Kennedy is the name.' The two men shook hands and Seán introduced Mary-Anne to him.

'Have you ever given thought to going into politics?' Pat Kennedy queried as the three of them strolled along the avenue.

'Never entered my head,' Seán laughed. 'I'm a schoolmaster, not a politician.'

'The Democratic Party could use the likes of you,' Pat Kennedy insisted. 'Your wife should encourage you to join,' and he smiled at Mary-Anne.

Mary-Anne was confounded at his assumption, and made haste to say that she was not Seán's wife.

'We are old neighbours and friends from back home in Galway,' she explained.

She turned to look at Seán and surprised a look of - was it disappointment or dismay? She was unable to decipher his expression, as it cleared in an instant.

'Yes,' Seán said, 'Mary-Anne was one of my pupils back home; her family are as my own family to me here in New York. She is my friend as I am hers,' he smiled at Mary-Anne as he spoke, his expression now clear and untroubled.

'I'll see you both at the next meeting then,' John Kennedy said as they parted on Lexington Avenue.

Mary-Anne and Seán walked on and chatted about the meeting they had just left, and she asked him about the other ones which he had attended previously.

'Were all those meetings to raise funds as well,

Seán,' she asked. 'Yes,' Seán replied. 'Actually, Mary-Anne, I must tell you something that you do not know about. I am a member of an organisation which acts in a sort of 'watchdog' capacity, in as much as there are some societies here which are all about gathering arms and plotting to get them over to the old country, so as to get another rebellion underway. I am at one with the bishops and priests in this instance. They feel that the primary aim of all good Irishmen and women should be the alleviation of the hunger, suffering and terrible diseases which are sweeping the country and killing thousands. There is a time and place for everything. Get the country strong and healthy first, feed and clothe the people, educate them, give them a pride in themselves, and then things will just naturally fall into place after that.'

'What kind of 'things' do you mean?' Mary-Anne queried.

'I mean that independence from Britain could happen before the next century if the people are strong, healthy and capable, and educated so as to go about achieving this with proper planning and advice.'

'You honestly believe that, Seán,' Mary-Anne asked.

'Yes, I do,' Seán spoke with conviction. 'I saw it myself in the Ballingarry fiasco. The men were too sick and hungry to fight, too desperate and racked with all kinds of diseases. They had the will, God help them, but, they just didn't have the physical strength for the endless miles of walking, the long hours without food, no shelter from the elements. The fighting was really over before it began.' He paused, 'The ones we were fighting against knew this before we ourselves did'. He shook his head, remembering.

'Do you want to hear all this again, Mary-Anne,' he asked. 'You know me when I start, I do forget that not everyone would be interested as much as myself.'

'Oh, I do want to hear whatever you want to tell me,' Mary-Anne said.

'The leaders were disgruntled with the behaviour of these poor unfortunates,' Seán went on, 'but they should not have expected these sick and starving men to have the same interest in achieving separation from England as they themselves had. God knows those men did their best at the time. Given another time in history when Ireland is healthy again, be it sooner or later, the aims of future leaders will possibly be achieved. But the brave few at Ballingarry will never be forgotten, they will go down in history, believe me, Mary-Anne.' Mary-Anne nodded her acquiescence and in her heart she firmly believed him.

# Four

Mary-Anne and Miss Janine sat comfortably in the cart as Beauty trotted her way around the park. The groom, Peter, sat on the back step as Miss Janine had decided that she would do the driving today, so he was temporarily off duty. It was a lovely day, the temperatures not yet reaching the unbearable proportions of July and August. The two girls wore cotton dresses and sun bonnets, Mary-Anne holding the parasol aloft to keep the heat of the sun away from the delicate skin of her charge. They bowled along, not a care in the world on either of them.

The new pony was arriving tomorrow and they were discussing the excitement of riding lessons and the purchasing of a stylish riding habit for Miss Janine. A name for this new arrival to the stables had also to be decided on, and the two of them tried to outdo each other in thinking up the most suitable name. Some of the names were wildly improbable and the two of them giggled happily and merrily together. Ah yes, life was good just now and was going to be even better in the future. Doctor and Mrs Wiseman were in the process of making arrangements for a trip to Europe for their daughter. The two girls spent the evenings perusing brochures and pinpointing ports of call on the large globe in the schoolroom. The little green dot that was Ireland on the western edge of Europe caused Mary-Anne's heart to miss a beat when she first located it. She placed the tip of her finger on it, closed her eyes and wished that sometime she could be planning her own trip to that little dot on the far side of the world. She did not, therefore, observe the soft smile on Miss Janine's face when that young lady noticed what Mary-Anne was doing.

Mary-Anne looked at the time piece pinned to the leather shelf in the front of the cart and reminded Miss Janine that they should be turning back and making their way home to Gramercy Avenue. Miss Janine checked Beauty, slowing her down, and on reaching a wider stretch of grass manoeuvred the cart to face for home.

As they neared the gate, the sound of clanging bells and the clattering of horses' hooves reached their ears.

'What is happening, Mary-Anne,' queried Miss Janine, 'there must be a parade of some sort going on out there.'

Peter interposed at that moment. 'Beg pardon, Miss, but that ringing of bells means there is an outbreak of fire somewhere and it must be close at hand.' Mary-Anne and her young mistress looked at each other, absolutely horrified. The word 'fire' struck horror into most people as many of the houses in the city and outskirts were constructed of wood, and an outbreak of fire could cause wholesale destruction in a very short space of time. People were constantly being warned, in the daily newspapers, from the pulpit, and by the police, of the danger of fire. Care must be taken at all times by those using open fires for any reason.

Mary-Anne recalled the words of a poem by St

Francis of Assisi, which Dad had often quoted to her, the Song of Brother Sun;

*Praise to thee my Lord, for Brother Fire*
*by whom thou lightest the night,*
*he is lovely and pleasant, mighty and strong ....*

Dado had always maintained that if fire was not kept under strict control it could quickly change from being 'lovely and pleasant' to being 'mighty and strong'.

The two girls, pale-faced, looked at each other, then Miss Janine clucked up Beauty and guided her in the direction of the park exit. As they reached the gate the clatter of horse hooves increased in volume, and sweeping around the corner they espied the wagon of the Hose Company. The four horses pulling it were straining under the weight of wagon and fire-fighters, the sweat matting their coats and flecks of foam from their open mouths dancing in the air around them. The men clung on to the hose restrainers, their brass helmets flashing in the sun.

The clamour of the bells was now deafening. People were running after the hose wagon, calling out for information, policemen on foot were hurrying in the direction taken by the wagon. The horse corps added to the general din as they clattered over the rough stony street in their wake.

Miss Janine handed over the reins to the groom, as she confessed she did not feel capable of driving through the cluttered streets just now. The two girls clutched each other for comfort, the need to get home to Gramercy the thought uppermost in their minds. They could smell smoke after they had travelled a short distance, a strong pungent aroma, borne on the slight breeze. Beauty was stepping out smartly, but the crowd was considerable by now, and the groom had to slow her down and negotiate with care through the throng.

They went down Amsterdam Avenue, across Templetin Street, and as they neared the garment district it became terrifyingly obvious that it was in this area the fire was centred.

There was a cordon of policemen preventing anyone from getting too close to the danger area. The groom suggested that the two girls remain in the cart and he would search for a possible detour away from the peril, and they then could travel that way.

It was a terrifying sight, the billowing smoke from the gaunt grey building, the flashes of flame to be seen through the small barred windows. Mary-Anne and Miss Janine were trembling with fear and terror; they couldn't go one way or the other, they were captive onlookers of the holocaust. Then Mary-Anne saw him, Tim O'Connor, pushing his way through the crowds towards them. 'Mary-Anne, for God's sake, what are you doing in this place, get out of here as fast as you can.' He gripped the reins and looked up at the two frightened girls. 'Miss Janine, you as well to be here, is there no one to look after the two of you?'

Mary-Anne told him that the groom was a short way off and would be back within minutes.

Just as she spoke a roar went up from the crowd gathered. The two girls and Tim looked towards the burning building and horror struck deep into their hearts at the sight which met their eyes. Women were clawing at the barred windows, their mouths stretched wide in soundless screams, the glow of the fire in stark contrast in the background. Tim turned back to the girls and said quietly, 'My worst fears are being realised.'

People were shouting and crying, 'Do something, get them out, help them'. Pandemonium reigned.

'Oh, Tim, what can be done for them,' Mary-Anne cried, as she clutched Tim's arm. 'God help them, God help them.'

'The fire-fighters are doing what they can,' Tim shouted above the din. 'There's a way around the back of that building, remember Mary-Anne? You and me saw it on one of our walks around here. I am going to go around that way and see if there is anything at all I can do.'

He looked at them, his eyes red rimmed from the smoke, his face blackened, but he smiled his cheerful smile, took a hand of each of them and pressing them tightly said, 'I can only try, wish me good luck, ladies.' He raised his hand in mock salute and pushed his way back through the crowd.

'Oh, Tim, don't, please Tim, come back, come back,' Mary-Anne screamed after him. Miss Janine joined her, pleading with him not to put himself in such danger, but the uniformed figure pushed his way resolutely and purposefully through the throng...the last sight the girls had of him from their vantage point in the pony cart was as he went around the side of the burning building.

Miss Janine was quiet, her eyes closed, her lips moving soundlessly, her hands pressed to her heart. With tears streaming down her face Mary-Anne repeated over and over again, 'Please God don't let anything happen to Tim, please God.'

The groom arrived back, breathless, grasped the pony's bridle, instructed Mary-Anne to hold on tightly to the reins, and by dint of hustling and bustling forced a path through the crowd. Beauty reared once or twice, but Mary-Anne, by now silent, held on grimly to the reins and eventually they reached a clearance. The groom jumped back into the cart and using the whip touched Beauty sharply on her flanks, and she stepped up to a gallop through the near empty streets.

Mary-Anne put her arms around Miss Janine and they both wept silently. They cried for the poor women and girls incarcerated in the doomed factory building, for the brave fire-fighters and policemen, and for Tim O'Connor, putting his own life in danger, in the hope of saving someone.

When they reached Gramercy Avenue the groom drove through the rear gates and bade the two girls to stay where they were while he hurried indoors for assistance for them. Matilda and Cook came rushing out, helped them down from the cart and bustled them indoors to the comfort of the kitchen. Stanley, the butler, came hurrying to enquire the cause of such commotion, and on being informed of the reason, he instructed that Cook give each of the young ladies a small taste of brandy.

'The horror they have witnessed this day will not be easily forgotten,' he stated. 'Get these young ladies to their beds immediately, and I will endeavour to contact the Master and Mistress.'

Mary-Anne was really grateful for the kindness and solicitude of the family retainers, but realised that her own care was for Miss Janine. Her own throat still smarted from the smoke inhaled at the scene of the fire, and she presumed that the same applied to her young charge.

'It is all right, Stanley,' she said, 'I am fine, and I must look after Miss Janine. She has been terribly distressed and upset at what we witnessed today. I must take care of her first.'

Miss Janine looked ready to faint, her face white and her eyes sunken deep in her head. Mary-Anne put her arms around her and Stanley went quickly ahead of them, opening the doors in their path. The two girls wearily ascended the wide staircase, their legs feeling so heavy, and it was a great effort for both of them to hold their skirts clear and climb aloft.

Miss Janine sank onto the daybed and closed her eyes. The slow tears trickled down her cheeks.

'Oh, Mary-Anne, these poor women, the fear and terror they are going through, it is unbelievable, and Tim, your friend Tim, will he be safe? Do you think he will, Mary-Anne?'

'Hush, Miss, hush,' Mary-Anne tried to comfort her. 'By now the firemen will have put out the fire, and Tim is a trained policeman, he knows what to do in cases like this.' In her heart she did not see how Tim could possibly live if he was caught in the fire, but knowing how brave and resourceful he was she prayed that he would survive. The smell of smoke lingered in their hair and on their clothes so Mary-Anne decided that Miss Janine should have a bath and then rest for a while in her room. She instructed Matilda when she came in answer to the bell to fill the bath in Miss Janine's room and to bring a light meal a little later for her following her bath.

Miss Janine, wearing a housecoat over her night-clothes, had regained some colour in her cheeks. She lay on the daybed and requested that Mary-Anne should massage her forehead with her favourite herbal oil.

'I will not sleep a wink tonight,' she declared. 'Every time I close my eyes the faces of those unfortunate women will come before me.'

'Never you mind, Miss, you will be asleep in no time,' Mary-Anne murmured as she smoothed the fragrant oils on the forehead of her young mistress.

Ten minutes later, Mary-Anne tiptoed out of the bedroom, closing the door quietly behind her. Her mistress was now sleeping, and she herself was beginning to react to the events of the day and could barely keep her eyes open. She would have a wash, a little lie down for half an hour or so, but just as she reached her bedroom door she heard Stanley call her name. 'Mary-Anne,' he called, 'your presence is required in the morning room, Master and Mistress have returned. They have been very involved down at the hospital with the casualties from the fire. However, they are very anxious to hear your account of the events in which you and Miss Janine were unwittingly involved.' He smiled at her and said 'come along when you are ready'.

# Five

Mary-Anne tidied her hair, passed the face flannel over her tired and grimy face, washed her hands and then went down the main stairs to the morning room.

She tapped at the door and on being summoned to enter went in. Doctor and Mrs Wiseman were seated close to the windows overlooking the gardens. Their pale and strained faces bore evidence of the travail which they had also been through.

'Good evening, Mary-Anne, how are you, and Miss Janine, how has she borne up under the awful experience of the fire,' asked Mrs Wiseman. She held out her hand to Mary-Anne. 'Come close, dear do, and tell Doctor and myself all about what befell you today.'

Her kindness and gentle tones were too much for Mary-Anne and to her own dismay she began to weep. Large tears ran down her face, and she struggled to find a handkerchief to wipe them away. All the horror of the afternoon came back to her, and she cried bitterly, hiccupping as she tried to apologise for her display of grief.

'Now, now, Mary-Anne,' Dr Wiseman said, 'a good cry will do you a world of good, do not worry about anything else, just cry yourself clean of all the terrible happenings of this day.' They both waited patiently until her tears ceased, encouraging her to sit down.

Mary-Anne, having explained that Miss Janine was now asleep, told her story of the day's events. How the two of them had gone out driving and had been unwittingly caught up in the fire drama, and been forced to witness the terrible sight of women screaming for help from behind barred windows. The firemen had been doing all they could. Then she told them about Tim O'Connor, her policeman friend, who had decided he was going to try to get into the building from the backway. Although both herself and Miss Janine had pleaded with him not to attempt it, he had gone ahead and the last they had seen of him was as he turned the corner of the burning building.

'Tim O'Connor,' Mrs Wiseman queried. 'He was a guest at Janine's party, was he not, a fine young man, most mannerly, as I recollect.'

'Yes Ma'am,' Mary-Anne said, 'he accompanied me that evening.'

'Mary-Anne, as you may know, Doctor and I have been at the hospital for the past many hours, assisting with the casualties from the fire,' Mrs Wiseman spoke wearily. 'It has been a most awful experience for everyone. There have been many deaths, terrible injuries, and a number of people unaccounted for. Several other buildings close to the factory also caught fire and hose companies had to come from as far away as Brooklyn to battle the flames.' She closed her eyes and rested her head on the back of her chair, and continued: 'everyone did their best, but the women really didn't have a chance. In this day and age to have bars on the windows and no proper exits is just unbelievable. This is a great country, but we still have so much to learn.'

'Maybe this tragedy will bring about changes in the

workplace,' Dr Wiseman said. 'God knows the people who own those factories live on the fat of the land, they are extremely wealthy people. I do believe they do not regard the people who work for them as human beings. No to them these workers are just a means to an end, to make money for them.' He sighed. 'The day will come when these employers will have to face the power of the people. Young, educated and energetic people will in the near future, call workers together to unite against this type of injustice in the work place, which is all too common. Changes will have to come about, will be forced to come about, in fact.' Mary-Anne nodded in agreement. So often had she listened to Seán Thornton as he spoke on these matters. This disastrous fire will have far-reaching effects, she thought.

'Have you eaten, Mary-Anne,' Mrs Wiseman enquired.

'No Ma'am, I am not hungry,' Mary-Anne replied, 'but when Miss Janine wakes and has supper, I will go to the kitchen and have something for myself then.'

Mrs Wiseman rose from her chair and said 'I will go upstairs and look in on my daughter. You go along to your room Mary-Anne, and rest. If Janine needs anything I will take care of it'. As she passed she patted Mary-Anne on her shoulders. 'Go along now, you are a good girl, we both appreciate your care and attention to our daughter.'

Mary-Anne thanked her employers and feeling the tears threaten again made haste to leave the room.

She closed her bedroom door behind her and rested

against it, her eyes closed. She thought of Tim and wondered where he was and if he was all right.

There was a gentle tap on the door and Mary-Anne called out, 'Who is it, please?'

'It is Seán, Mary-Anne, Seán Thorton.' At the sound of his voice Mary-Anne's heart leaped. 'May I speak with you?' Mary-Anne opened wide her door and when she saw Seán standing there she went straight to the comfort of his arms and rested her weary head on his shoulder. She did not see the expression on his face, or feel the feather light kiss he touched to her red curls, she only knew that she was at peace, and the horrors of the day receded for this time at least.

As Mary-Anne finished telling Seán the story of the fire she noticed his grim expression as he spoke forcefully. ''Tis very wrong that factory owners are getting away with this carry-on, locking people in during working hours, windows and doors barred, it is downright disgraceful.'

Mary-Anne had to agree with him: to the end of her days she would remember the sight of those women desperately tearing at the bars which were preventing their escape.

'Tim always says the same,' she said. 'He told me that he used to have nightmares about this happening.' The full force of where he was and what might have happened to Tim came back to her and she grabbed Seán's arm. 'Oh, Seán, how can we find out about Tim, if he is alright? I'm so worried about him'.

'You think a lot of Tim O'Connor, don't you Mary-Anne,' Seán queried, a strange expression on his face.

'Yes, yes, I do, he is such fun and we have had

lovely days out together,' Mary-Anne assured him. 'He gets very low in himself at times, missing his mam and dad and his family. He went to my dad for his permission and we go out one day a week. We go to see the sights of the city, he always says he wants me to get to know New York ....' Mary-Anne realised that she was chattering on at a great rate and stopped.

Seán remarked in a quiet tone, his face expressionless, 'would you two be on for marrying, do you think?'

Mary-Anne felt that she wanted to laugh - marry Tim? No at all, the only person she would want to marry, if and when the right time came, was the man standing beside her. She opened her mouth to say this and stopped. How could she say to Master Thornton that she would like to marry him, he being her old schoolmaster - he would probably laugh at her, it was foolish to even be thinking about it. She hesitated and then said, 'It is not right to be talking like this, Tim could be dead'. She began to feel angry with Seán.

'You haven't answered my question,' Seán persisted.

'No, and I don't want to,' Mary-Anne retorted angrily. 'Tim could be badly hurt, or even dead.' Her voice quivered 'this is not the time to be speaking about such things'.

Seán made a visible effort to calm himself, drawing a deep breath, and said, 'I am sorry, Mary-Anne, it is wrong of me to have said what I did. I apologise to you'.

Mary-Anne glanced at him and observed a brief glimpse of sadness on his face before he smiled at her.

She smiled back at him and the anger which had surged through her a short time ago now vanished.

'Seán, how will we find out where Tim is and how things are with him?' she asked. 'Both Miss Janine and myself are so anxious about him. You know we tried to stop him going back to find a way out for the women, but he just went away and wouldn't listen to us.'

'I'll go to the nearest precinct straight away,' Seán said. 'I'll make enquiries, they're bound to know the full story of the fire by now. Don't you worry your head about it, with the help of God he is safe and well.'

# Six

When Seán went back to the schoolroom Mary-Anne
returned to her bedroom, and sat down on her bed.
Her mind was in a whirl, she was so terribly worried
about Tim O'Connor. She could not grasp the fact
that she might never see him again, never laugh at his
antics, go on walking trips around New York, visit
Frau Gruber's tea rooms to sit and talk all about home
with him. He was her friend, her pal and without him
her life would be a lonely one. But tonight she had
realised something for the first time, and that was
that Seán Thornton was the one man that she would
like to marry, he was her true love, and if she was
ever to marry anyone it would be Seán. She felt sad
and unhappy as she knew that Seán regarded her as a
child, a former pupil of his, he was her schoolmaster,
and he most certainly did not think of her as anything
other than a child. 'I wish I had someone to talk to
about my problem,' she thought. 'I can't bother Miss
Janine, she wouldn't want to be listening to me
romancing about him, she is fond of him herself.' She
left her bedroom and went along to check her charge,
she could be awake by now. She tapped lightly on the
door, opened it and went in. Miss Janine was still
asleep, her face had not regained its colour, and every
now and again a sob shook her slight frame. As
Mary-Anne bent over her to tuck the comforter more
closely around her, she roused slightly and Mary-
Anne heard her say faintly, 'Tim, Tim, come back,

come back' before she sank back into a deeper sleep.

Mary-Anne closed her own eyes and prayed earnestly that Tim was safe. She thought of his family at home in Kerry, who depended on him so much, and who, at this time, did not know about the awful situation in which he was now involved.

As Seán Thornton strode along the Avenue making his way to Precinct 36, his thoughts were, to say the least, chaotic. He was annoyed with himself for the way in which he had spoken to Mary-Anne. Now that he had cooled down a bit he could understand why she should be so upset about Tim O'Connor. He had met Tim on one or two occasions since the birthday party for Miss Janine, and he had enjoyed his company. The two of them had actually got on very well together, their love for Ireland forming a strong bond between them and their political ideas very similar.

His anger, as he could now realise, had been caused by the feelings which he himself now had for Mary-Anne. Since he had come to the United States and renewed acquaintance with the Joyce family, he had begun to view Mary-Anne in a totally different way than on a pupil to teacher basis. She was no longer the gaunt, hungry child whom he had helped to reach the *Clarence*, four or so years ago, when the family were leaving Ireland for the brave new world of America. No, Mary-Anne was now a young lady, bright and quick of mind, beautiful with her clear complexion, deep blue eyes and copper coloured hair. He smiled to himself as he remembered how Mary-Anne viewed the sprinkling of freckles across her nose, with something less than delight, it must be said. She was a lovely girl now, but she did not regard him as anything other than her former schoolmaster. Certainly she looked kindly on Tim O'Connor, and Seán had no way of knowing how Tim himself regarded Mary-Anne. He was troubled by his own feelings for Mary-Anne, and wondered what the future held for both of them. He roused himself from these worrying thoughts and concentrated on locating the local precinct which he believed was somewhere in the general direction in which he was heading. As he turned the corner onto the next street he observed a crowd gathered at the front of a brownstone building half way down the street, and quickened his steps. This was the 36th Precinct, and the place where he might be able to get information on the whereabouts of Tim O'Connor.

Janine Wiseman opened her eyes and turning her head towards the window, observed that it was coming on for evening time. There was no sound in the house. She was glad of the quiet as she wanted to think about the events of the day, terrible and all as they were, before people came to fuss and bustle about her. While she had been asleep she had had a dream. She and Tim O'Connor had been climbing a steep hill together, the crown of which reached into the clouds. Although she had not ever been to Ireland, she fancied that - there being so much green everywhere, grass, trees, hedges, so many shades of green - this was Ireland. So often had Mary-Anne described the beauty of the Irish countryside to her that her subconcious had taken everything in and even her dreams were coloured with the green of Ireland. Tim had been holding her hand and encouraging her in the difficult climb 'Come along, girlie, you're doing fine, we'll reach the top together, only a short way now.' She had protested and pleaded tiredness, but he wouldn't listen to her. 'Hold onto me, alanna, I've enough strength for the two of us,' he laughed down at her, his eyes alight with mischief. They reached the summit and observed the world below them, people, animals and wagons dashing hither and thither. Tim had turned to her and said, 'This is the best place to be, you can look into your heart and know what is real, high up here away from everyone'. Then she had awakened, the dream fading. Her hand was still reaching out for Tim's hand when she awoke, the dream was so vivid.

Tim had been very much on her mind before she had fallen asleep, and had evidently invaded her dreams. Was there any significance in such a dream, she wondered. Then the full impact of the horror of the day came back to her, her teeth chattered and shivers of fear shook her body. She reached for the bellpush and tugged it several times.

Mary-Anne hastened up the stairway. It was as if Miss Janine was not ever going to let go of the bellpush: the clang from it followed her up the stairs as she sped along towards her mistress's room. She knocked and quickly entered the room. Miss Janine was sitting up in bed, her hand still clutching the bell cord, and she looked quite agitated.

'Yes, Miss, here I am,' Mary-Anne said. 'Are you all right?'

'Yes, Mary-Anne, I am feeling quite well, but still fearful of that dreadful fire. Tell me, have you any word about the same fire and about your friend,

Tim?' Miss Janine spoke urgently.

'Not yet, Miss,' Mary-Anne replied, 'I was speaking with Master Thornton, and he has gone to the nearest precinct to find out whatever he can.'

'Oh, good,' Miss Janine said. 'But, Mary-Anne, I must tell you, I had a dream. Tim was in it, we were climbing a steep hill somewhere in Ireland - it had to be Ireland, so much green everywhere ....' She proceeded to tell Mary-Anne about it, and when she had finished, Mary-Anne had to agree that it was indeed a peculiar sort of dream, but, thankfully, not an upsetting one. The two girls were quiet for a time, each thinking her own thoughts, then Miss Janine said, 'Mary-Anne, will you come with me to get whatever information we can about the fire and its consequences?'

'Oh, yes, certainly, Miss, I'll go along with you,' Mary-Anne agreed. 'But, perhaps, we should wait a little while, Master Seán may have some news for us. He has been gone for some time now.'

'Yes, perhaps, another half an hour or so,' Miss Janine agreed, 'but if he has not arrived back by then, you and I will set out together to find out whatever we can.' Mary-Anne was relieved at the delay as she was rather anxious about travelling through the city at this time of the evening, and she decided to enlist the opinion of Stanley about the advisability of their doing so. He might have an alternative suggestion to make.

'I will leave you for a short time, Miss,' she said. 'I have a small chore to take care of before we go out.'

Stanley was somewhat dubious about the proposed outing. 'New York is not a safe city to travel through in the evening hours, Mary-Anne,' he said. 'I know how anxious you must be, and young Miss Janine can get ideas into her head which can be difficult to change, but my advice to you is, be guided in this matter by your own common sense as the Master and Mistress have returned to the hospital and are not here to ask their opinion. However, if Mr Thornton returns soon the matter will be resolved.'

Mary stood at the window overlooking the street and was thus able to observe Seán when he rounded the corner and walked up towards the main door. He looked troubled, his head bent, and he appeared lost in thought. As he neared the main door, he glanced up at the windows and observed Mary-Anne's anxious face. For a brief moment as the two young people looked at each other, their feelings were evident on their faces, then Mary-Anne glanced away, her cheeks reddening. Seán Thornton hurriedly reminded himself that the expression he had observed on her face was only, 'wishful thinking' on his part. 'Keep a cool head, Seán a mhic' he told himself, as he turned the door key and let himself into the house.

# Seven

Tim O'Connor was suffering from smoke inhalation but otherwise was unharmed, so Seán informed the two worried girls. He had succeeded in rescuing three of the women through the back door of the factory. These women had been working in the kitchen area and had therefore more freedom of movement than the other unfortunates. There had been one fatality among the fire fighters, and one policeman so badly injured by falling masonry that he was not expected to live beyond the night. An Irishman by the name of Thomas Hayden, a young lad from Kildare, he had been endeavouring to climb up to the windows when a piece of concrete became dislodged and knocked him to the ground, where he was in direct line of another large piece when it also crashed down. Seán imparted all the knowledge he had gleaned within the precinct to the two girls as they sat in the morning room. Relief that Tim was safe, sorrow for the dead and dying warred within Mary-Anne's mind. Thank God that Tim is safe, she thought. Poor Thomas Hayden, I wonder does Tim know him.

Aloud she asked Seán which hospital Tim was in, and when could he have visitors.

'He is in St Camillus on 86th street. He'll be there for a day or two, as they say his lungs are in a bad way' Seán answered. 'I do not know the visiting times, but there'll be so many ill people there after the fire that I can't see how there'll be any hard and fast rules on visitors coming and going for the next few days at any rate.'

Mary-Anne looked at Miss Janine, and it was evident the same thought had come into both of their minds. Miss Janine spoke for the two of them.

'We will go to see him this evening. Will you accompany us, Mr Thornton,' she asked pleadingly. 'Mama and Papa are not at home at present, but I am sure that they would not object to us going as far as 86th street, provided you are with us.'

Seán glanced at Mary-Anne, and from her expression it was obvious that she was of the same mind as Miss Janine.

'I will be glad to travel with you both to the hospital, it will give me an opporutnity to visit with Tim also,' Seán said. 'We should leave shortly, could you be ready in twenty minutes?'

The two girls hurried upstairs to dress for going outside, and were down in the hallway a few minutes short of the allotted time. It was a long walk to the hospital, there were no hansom cabs plying their trade on the route which they travelled, and it was a tired trio who reached the main entrance to the hospital an hour or so later. In the cool foyer there were many people milling around, the nurses distinguished by their uniforms, and the rattling of their rosary beads preceded the Holy Sisters as they moved calmly but purposefully about their business. Seán enquired as to where Tim O'Connor could be found and the three of them went in the direction indicated.

Tim was lying in a darkened room, his eyes closed.

He looked pale and unwell, but as Mary-Anne touched his hand lying on the counterpane his eyes opened immediately. They focused on Mary-Anne and a hint of a smile crossed his face. 'Well, if it isn't Miss Mary-Anne Joyce,' he whispered hoarsely, 'How did you find your way to this place?' He then realised that she was not alone, and said 'I am the lucky man to have so many visitors'. He tried to sit up, but a bout of coughing shook his frame, and he gratefully lay back when Seán assisted him to do so.

Mary-Anne felt a bit shy seeing Tim in this situation and was unsure about conversing with him, and she was indeed grateful when Seán chatted to him about the fire, and the changes which could ensue from the days devastation. Tim answered him in monosyllables, as the effort of speaking more than a few words at a time rendered him quite breathless. When Miss Janine approached the bed he reached for her hand and whispered,' May I have the next waltz?' The two girls began to laugh, covering their mouths to stifle the sound, and Seán grinned in appreciation of the joke. There was no doubt about it, Tim was a likeable person and any feelings of dislike or distrust which he had ever harboured about Tim faded away.

A pleasant few minutes passed between the four friends and when it was time to leave for the long walk home Mary-Anne promised Tim that they would call again very soon. She enquired if there was anything in particular he might want which they could get for him. He shook his head and mouthed 'No thank you'. He was obviously tired out at this stage, and when Mary-Anne glanced back as she reached the door his eyes were closed and his expression peaceful.

She felt a great uplift in her spirits. Tim was alive and would hopefully get completely better. Seán was also happy and cheerful, and appeared to have forgotten his earlier problems about Tim, and Miss Janine, although quite tired, was walking along, a dreamy look on her face, humming the air of the 'Blue Danube'. Worn out by the eventful day, the two girls retired to their beds early and both slept undisturbed.

# Eight

The headlines of the newspapers on the following days screamed for changes in the 'sweatshops' of the garment industry. Twenty-two women had died in the fire, and many more were badly injured. These included firefighters and policemen. Tim O'Connor was featured as the 'Young Irish officer from the 36th Precinct who had endangered his own life while trying to rescue some of the trapped women'. His bravery was acclaimed by his superior officers. The seriously ill officer, Thomas Hayden, had not regained consciousness, and there was little hope of his recovering from the terrible injuries which he had received.

That same day Mary-Anne went home to visit her parents in Coburg Street. She had a mixture of feelings as she read about the fearful events of the previous day in her dad's newspaper. She was proud of Tim, sorry for the relatives and friends of the dead and dying, angry at the greed and stupidity of the owners of the gutted factory. She had a discussion with Mam and Dad, and they were of the same mind as herself. Her mam was upset about Tim and his serious injury, 'Lung trouble is bad,' she maintained. 'It'll be a long time clearing up, a foolish lad, but brave beyond words.'

Dad argued that smoke inhalation and 'lung trouble' were not one and the same. 'He'll be over it in no time at all,' he said, 'sure he is as strong as an ox, that young fella me lad. In no time at all he'll be out and about again, tormenting us all with his carry-on.' It was obvious how much her mam and dad thought of Tim O'Connor, Mary-Anne thought to herself.

During dinner Mary-Anne mentioned the meeting which she and Seán attended in the Fraoch Bán Inn, and asked her parents if they would help in the fund raising events. They were happy to help in whatever way they could. Mary-Anne then told them about the two men who had been at the meeting and who had not liked it one bit when Seán Thornton had objected to the direction in which the discussions were heading.

'There are a lot of hot heads around at present,' Dad agreed, 'all fired up with thoughts of liberating Ireland.'

Mam interposed, 'Don't *you* get involved, Mary-Anne, Master Seán is more than able to take care of himself'.

Mary-Anne agreed that he was, 'but I can still see how they looked at him when he spoke up from the floor'.

'Aye, that's as may be, but you keep your distance, alanna,' Mam said. 'Us Irish are far too fond of getting into debates and arguments. Keep a cool head and you'll never get into trouble, mark my words.'

'The Young Irelanders who have escaped to this land are looking for revenge and crying out for revolution,' Dad maintained. 'They are trying to encourage the Irish and Americans of Irish descent to fight to free Ireland and wreak vengeance on the Sasannach!' He puffed his pipe and continued, 'When the time is right success will follow'.

'But, Dad, aren't you afraid that we might all get too comfortable over here and forget all that is going on at home,' Mary-Anne asked.

''Tis true for you, a stóir,' Dad agreed, 'and that is something to remind people of when you are organising and fund-raising. The money is to be used to buy food for the people to give them back their right to life, that should never be forgotten. We all must help those who cannot help themselves.'

As Mary-Anne walked along the street on her way back to Gramercy Avenue, she observed two gentlemen approaching. They looked vaguely familiar, but she could not recollect where or when she had seen them before. As they neared her one of them glanced her way and nudged his companion, and as she passed them by he said to her 'You are a friend of that trouble-maker Thornton, aren't you?' Mary-Anne was so shocked that she stopped and looked at them in dismay. Normally she would have ignored the passing comments of young men which she was occasionally subjected to if she were unescorted, but this was not a light-hearted remark, this remark was laced with venom.

'I beg your pardon,' she stammered.

'You heard me,' he said. 'Tell him from us we do not want his kind involved in what we are trying to do.'

Mary-Anne was so dumbfounded that she could not say one word, and it was only when they had passed on their way that she continued on her way.

She was really frightened and hurried the rest of her journey to Gramercy Avenue. She hastened indoors to locate Seán, but Stanley informed her that he had left an hour or so ago. Mary-Anne recalled now where she had seen these men before. It was at the meeting in the Fraoch Ban establishment, and they had both been on the dais to the rear of the front table.

Seán and she were to meet up with Pat Kennedy the following evening at the entrance to the emporium. She felt extremely nervous about the next meeting to be held there. What would those men do when Seán arrived, would they threaten him, might they even attack him? Mary-Anne did not sleep at all well that night. Her imagination ran away with her as she visualised the danger Seán could be in, the possible hand-to-hand fighting that could take place. By the morning she was pale with exhaustion.

'My gracious, Mary-Anne,' exclaimed Miss Janine when Mary-Anne arrived to begin her day's work, 'you look worn out, what have you been doing?'

'I did not sleep very well, Miss, I have things on my mind,' Mary-Anne explained.

'Oh really, what "things," dear Mary-Anne, do tell me,' coaxed Miss Janine.

It was a relief for Mary-Anne to tell her story to her mistress, and that young lady was quite incensed when she finished her tale.

'Well, that is a nice how-do-you-do, I must say,' she exclaimed. 'Of course you must inform Master Thornton at once.'

'You do not have lessons this morning, Miss, you recall you are visiting with your Aunt Sophie,' Mary-Anne reminded her. 'So it will not be possible for me to see Master Thornton until this evening. He will be calling to take me to this fund-raising meeting at seven o'clock.'

'Oh, that is true, it slipped my mind,' Miss Janine sighed. 'Aunt Sophie does not come to New York often, so Mama has decreed that I must visit with her. Such a pity it has to be today.'

Mary-Anne heartily agreed. She was anxious to speak with Seán, and warn him that there could be trouble ahead for him. Now she would have to contain herself until the coming evening.

# Nine

Pat Kennedy was waiting for them outside the entrance door into the Fraoch Bán. Mary-Anne was glad to see him as she considered that he would be of assistance to Seán should the need arise. Seán himself did not appear to be bothered by the information she had passed on to him about the two men who had accosted her.

'Pay no heed to the likes of those two, Mary-Anne,' he said when she told him her story. 'All talk and no action. When you face up to bullies, which those two are, they usually draw back and that is the end of it. I'm just sorry that you were accosted by them.'

But when Mary-Anne glanced up at Seán she realised that he was very angry, his voice was quiet and controlled but his eyes were bleak and cold.

'Were you upset by this, Mary-Anne,' he asked.

Mary-Anne admitted that she had been quite frightened. When Pat Kennedy heard the story his reaction was similar to Seán's.

'The cause those people espouse will not be helped by that type of carry-on,' he said. 'The best way to deal with this is to ignore it.'

The three of them entered the meeting room and took their seats half-way up the room. Dick O'Connell and James Morgan were already seated and across the dais to their left were the two men who had spoken to Mary-Anne on the previous say. She felt a cold chill pass through her when she encountered the eyes of one of them. There was no apparent recognition, but she observed that he drew the attention of his companion to their presence in the hall.

The meeting came to order and various people began to put forward suggestions, and arrangements already made since the last meeting, were confirmed.

Mary-Anne had spent a lot of her free time in writing down ideas which she had about ways and means of raising money. She had one thought in particular, which she had mentioned to Seán as they had travelled to the meeting and he had agreed that it certainly was worth putting forward for consideration. When James Morgan asked if there were any other suggestions to be put before the table, Mary-Anne, gathering her courage, raised her hand and was given permission to speak.

'My suggestion is as follows,' she said, and proceeded to say that there could be an open air gathering, a Lá Ceoil, in the great park close to the city centre. 'There are many musicians, singers and dancers living in New York and around who I feel would be delighted to take part in such a concert. Everyone would volunteer their services - baking, and demonstrations of various kinds.' Mary-Anne was nervous and her voice shook a little, but she continued on, saying that the many better-off Irish, be they shopkeepers or tradespeople, might be interested in having their company names displayed throughout the park, for a worthwhile contribution to the fund-raising efforts.

When she resumed her seat there was a burst of applause and a great buzz of talk throughout the room.

'Your name, young lady?' James Morgan rapped on the table for order. 'Your suggestion is an excellent one. It will take a great deal of organising, of course, but many hands make light work and I believe that this planned concert can be successfully carried out.'

'I am Mary-Anne Joyce, from the County Galway,' Mary-Anne replied. 'I am pleased that you like my suggestion.'

'Would you be willing to help organise this fleadh,' James Morgan asked. 'It is your idea, after all,' he smiled at her.

'I will do whatever I can,' Mary-Anne smiled back at him.

'Committees will have to be set up, as I consider if this suggestion is followed through properly a lot of money could be raised. And, may I say,' he continued, 'it will be a great opportunity for our musicians, singers and dancers to get together. It could be an annual event.' From the enthusiastic reaction of the audience it was obvious that many more were in accord with him.

There was a break in the meeting at this point and many of the attendance came forward to shake Mary-Anne's hand, and congratulate her.

'My wife is a sean-nós singer,' one man said. 'She rarely gets a chance to sing, I know she'd be delighted to help out.'

'I'm a piper,' another man said, 'I'd be only too glad to take part. Piping is a lonely way of making music at the best of times, but this way I'd be with many of the same and we'd have a great time.'

'I am a Clare man,' a grey-haired man spoke.

'Traditional music is my life, and the fiddle my instrument, count me in to help.' Mary-Anne was amazed at the reception her idea was getting, and was delighted with herself.

Seán and Pat Kennedy were chatting together towards the rear of the room, waiting for Mary-Anne. She was flushed and excited when she joined them.

'Congratulations on a superb idea,' Pat Kennedy shook her hand. 'It will appeal to many people and it is a great opportunity for the Irish to get together for a bit of a céilí, a very large céilí, we hope.'

Seán laughed and said, 'I might be tempted to play a few tunes myself'.

'If there's a prize for the best singer I might enter for that,' Pat Kennedy grinned. 'I do sing a few bars now and again.'

When the meeting resumed committees were selected for the various fund-raising plans and Mary-Anne, Pat and Seán found themselves co-opted onto the Lá Ceoil committee. There was a considerable amount of arranging to be sorted out before the Lá could be considered a definite happening.

Applications for the use of the park, and whatever other legalities needed clarifying would have to be sorted out before any other plans could be set in motion. A date would have to be set and the sooner the committee swung into action the better. There was general agreement from the floor.

At the conclusion of the meeting, Mary-Anne, Seán and Pat Kennedy decided they would call to visit with Tim O'Connor, as the hospital was but a few blocks away from the Fraoch Bán. When they reached his ward they found him sitting out on a chair. His colour was still bad, but his voice, when he greeted them, was almost back to normal. He was very pleased with the idea of the Lá Ceoil. 'The prayers we said in the cathedral were answered,' he grinned at Mary-Anne. 'When I get out of here I'll start to practise some of the old scéals for ye.'

Mary-Anne studied him when he was chatting with Seán and Pat and could see a great improvement in his condition. His eyes were not as bright as usual, and it was obvious that his chest was not completely clear, but the Tim O'Connor of old was slowly but surely coming back to normal. Tears threatened as Mary-Anne remembered the chances he had taken during the dreadful fire, but she blinked them away. When they were leaving he reached for her hand, and said 'Come again soon, Mary-Anne, I do be lonesome on and off'.

She promised that she would and he said, 'don't forget her ladyship as well'. Mary-Anne laughed. 'I'll tell Miss Janine you were asking after her.'

'Aye, do that,' Tim said with a smile, 'I'll be watching out for the two fine lassies, don't you forget now.'

When they reached the door Mary-Anne looked back. Tim was looking after them. She gave him a little wave, and had to giggle when he impudently blew her a kiss. She felt happy again.

# Ten

One hot morning in late July, Mary-Anne was summoned to visit her parents and uncle and aunt at Coburg Street. The newsboy, who delivered the daily newspaper to Gramercy Avenue had requested that this message be passed to Mary-Anne, as he handed in the newspaper to Stanley. On receiving the message Mary-Anne went to Miss Janine's bedroom to seek permission to leave the house for a couple of hours.

'Why do your Mama and Papa wish to see you, Mary-Anne,' Miss Janine enquired.

'I do not know, Miss,' Mary-Anne answered, 'there might be some news from Ireland, or there may be some other reason. May I have permission to leave?'

'Why, of course you may,' Miss Janine said. 'Mary-Anne, do you know that I have never sat down to tea with your family, in your home?' She sounded plaintive, and Mary-Anne had to smile at her.

'You know Miss that Coburg Street is quite a way from here. Would you be up to walking that distance, do you think?'

'I could use the dog-cart, Beauty would welcome the exercise,' Miss Janine said eagerly. 'It would be good to get outdoors in this hot weather. The heat is excessive indoors, and I do yearn to be out in the air even for a short time.

'But, perhaps, they do not wish to have a visit from me, but only from you today?' Miss Janine looked anxiously at Mary-Anne.

'No, Mam, and Dad too, and Aunt Bina are known to your mama from years back,' Mary-Anne insisted. 'Do come along, Miss, it will make a change for you. The weather has been so sultry and so tiring and uncomfortable, that a trip in the open air as far as Coburg Street would suit you nicely.'

Miss Janine did not need a lot of coaxing, and in no time at all she had given instructions that Beauty be harnessed and the dogcart brought around to the front of the house, while she dressed for the outing.

Mary was pleased that Miss Janine was anxious to visit with her mam and dad, and Uncle Arthur and Aunt Bina. She had never considered inviting Miss Janine to her home as she did not think it appropriate that her young mistress should do so. Then, recalling that this was America and not Ireland, where the wealthy did not fraternize with their servants, Mary-Anne was very happy that this visit was happening.

The planning and preparation for the Lá Ceoil, to be held on September 7th, was going along very well. It was time-consuming and left Mary-Anne with little time to herself, so she was glad of the respite and she was looking forward to seeing her parents. She was happy that her own family were taking such an interest in the festival and like the other people involved were putting their hearts and souls into making it a successful venture. Everything, so far, was progressing satisfactorily.

For the outing, Miss Janine wore a pretty pink cotton gown, and a white bonnet trimmed with a pink ribbon. Her shoes were of soft white kid, and she carried a white and pink parasol. Mary-Anne wore a pale green muslin gown with a white sash. Her white straw bonnet was trimmed with daisies, and she wore dainty black patent shoes. Her skin was lightly tanned and the freckles across her nose had increased in number from the summer sun. Setting off in the dog-cart with Peter in attendance they presented a very pretty picture in the July sunshine. The faint breeze occasioned by the movement of the dog-cart as Beauty trotted along, was very pleasant, and the two young ladies used their fans as well, to keep them cool on their journey.

Reaching Coburg Street some forty minutes later the two girls were warmly welcomed by Mam and Dad, and ushered into the room where they were relieved of their bonnets and parasols. Aunt Bina had not yet arrived, so Mam brought the two girls some cooling drinks which they gladly accepted. Miss Janine felt it quite easy to carry on a conversation with Mary-Anne's parents. Bina, when she arrived, was delighted to meet her, as she remembered her as a babe in arms, visiting the house with her mama, where Bina worked as a lady's maid.

The reason for the request to come home was explained when Honor and Jamesy told Mary-Anne that the paperwork for their small holding in the Catskill region had been completed and the cabin and land were now officially theirs. They were so pleased with their good news that Mary-Anne hid her own sadness at the thought of them leaving New York, and she hugged her mam and dad in delight.

'This is wonderful news,' she said. 'You have waited so long for this, Mam and Dad. When are you planning to leave here?'

'It will be before Christmas, we think,' Honor said. 'Dad will work on with Arthur for a few more months - it isn't easy to get good farriers at this time of year - and maybe, by then Arthur will have news of his own farm.' She was flushed and happy and looked years younger, as did Jamesy; their dream was being realised at long last.

Mary-Anne looked at her mam and dad and thought to herself how fine they looked. She knew that her mam had been married when she was eighteen years old, and Jamesy had been twenty-two. She had been born two years later. She worked out in her mind that Mam was a couple of years away from forty, and Dad just forty-two. Her mam's hair was a lovely soft brown, and her dad's the same, but with a hint of auburn, and they both had blue eyes and fresh complexions. The past few years spent living in fairly good conditions and eating healthy food had cleared the sallow tinge from their skins and brought back the shine to their eyes and hair. That they loved each other was quite apparent, and they were never too shy to display their affection for each other. Mary-Anne had been reared in a happy home, surrounded by the love of her parents and grandparents. They had sustained each other through the bad times in Ireland, and Mary-Anne often wished Mamo and Dado could have had the comfort in their lives that Mam and Dad and she now had. Never a night went by that she did not remember them, and all her friends who had died and were buried back home in Ireland, in her prayers.

Mam and Dad now had their chance to go back to farming which was the life to which they had been reared. It would be hard enough work preparing the ground, Dad explained, it had never been tilled and was overgrown with brushwood. Their lawyer, Henry Durcan, who had come out from Mayo many years before, had explained to them about the problems pertaining to their new farm, but he believed that it had great potential. There would be more than spadework involved in bringing it to a good fertile level, he had advised them. He was interested in the Joyce family and in their adventurous undertaking, and he went so far as to procure books for them which would provide guidance about many aspects of farming in this country with which they would not be familiar.

Arthur and Bina had not as yet finalised their purchase of the small farm located in the same area in the Catskills. Negotiations were proceeding and they believed that it would be a matter of weeks before they would get the final word. It was a happy gathering that day in the Coburg Street apartment, and Miss Janine was delighted that Mary-Anne had insisted that she should accompany her to her home.

After their meal, the women cleared away and Dad and Uncle Arthur, puffing away at their pipes, settled back to read the Irish-American newspapers.

'Be the hokey,' Arthur exclaimed a minute or so later, 'Would you believe it, the Queen of England is to make a visit to Ireland - it says so here in the newspaper.' Glancing around at his attentive audience, he continued, 'Queen Victoria is to visit the cities of Cork and Dublin in Ireland in the month of August. She requests that the visit be without any state or expense, and that there be no banquets. She wishes as many people as is possible to be given the opportunity to see her. She will travel by special carriage, which is already under construction in Dublin. She would like a *cortège* to be arranged, similar to that at Ascot, so that this can be realised'.

'Well, that bates all,' declared Dad, when he had finished. 'Shure there's no money in the country to feed the people let alone build a special carriage or arrange a *cortège*, whatever that means.'

Mam agreed. 'Isn't the entire country in a shocking state? Where is the money to come from for this, I ask myself? But, I have to say that I'd like the chance to see the Queen myself,' she smiled a little shamefacedly at the family. 'She is quite young, you know, about thirty years, and already has a few in the family. She had collections made throughout England, I heard from someone, to get money to send to Ireland.'

'It might be a blessing in disguise, this visit,' Bina remarked. 'The young Queen will see for herself the state the country is in. She might keep a better eye on those she has in charge of Ireland, and make some changes. God works in mysterious ways, you know.'

'Aye, 'tis true for you, Bina,' Dad said. 'Good luck to her anyway, she's only young, and her position in life isn't an easy one.'

# Eleven

A very busy was time ahead for everyone involved in the new fund-raising efforts. The stories coming back from Ireland were as bad as ever, and it was urgent that help be sent as quickly as possible to the Famine victims.

The response to the appeals for help in organising and running the various events was wonderful. An advertisement was inserted in the Irish-American newspapers giving details of the many fund-raising efforts being got underway. The Lá Ceoil got front page coverage, and people who wished to take part on this great occasion were asked to contact the committees at the Fraoch Bán establishment.

One of the suggestions put forward for the big day was that an area should be set aside in the field for displays of traditional craft work, such as lace-making, basket weaving, crochet, knitting, *petit-point*, quilting, and other crafts. Another section would be given over to cheese making, soda bread baking, rasp - a traditional potato and flour cake - and gruel making.

When Mary-Anne next called home to visit with her mam and dad, she found the place a hubbub of activity. Her parents were busily working on various schemes and designs for the Lá Ceoil; a few of the neighbours were also in the house, fingers flying as they plied their needles.

'The best idea that's been thought up in many's the

long day,' Dad maintained. 'You've never seen such industry about the place. No one has time to hang about and talk, they're all flitting here and there, doin' this and that. The singers and musicians are gathering for practices in whatever house they can. It's a long time since I've seen people so occupied and content in themselves.' Even as he was speaking he was nailing together the makings of a stool.

Mary-Anne busied herself making a meal for all these industrious people, and marvelled to herself at how willing people were to help a worthy cause. After the meal her fingers itched to do some work herself, and she gratefully accepted threads and needles from her mam, with instructions to do 'some of the grand lacework your Mamo taught you, alannah'.

Mary-Anne decided that she would suggest to Miss Janine that perhaps her mother and her friends might consider coming to the park to purchase some of the lovely craft work which would be on display there. Irish lace and crochet were world famous and this would be a great opportunity to purchase some, and also to watch the women as they worked on their craft.

A lot of arranging needed to be done. Permission had been granted from the city council for the use of the south field in the park. Conditions had been set out which must be rigidly adhered to. No alcohol was to be available, and the noise level to be kept to a minimum. Order must be maintained at all times during the day, and the field was to be cleared of garbage and left in a spotless condition at the end of the day.

The men of the local hose companies, many of them native-born Irish, volunteered their assistance in whatever way they could be of service.The officers and men of the local precincts were also glad to help in the great fund-raising affair. There was a hum of excitement about the place. People who had never made any effort to integrate into the life of the new country in which they now lived, came forward to help and many of them had suggestions about the festival which had not been heard previously. Life in the Irish ghettos had taken on a different aspect, even if it was only for a short time.

There was a four week preparation time set out and an enormous amount of work had to be done within that time. Seán Thornton paid a visit to the bishop's palace to ask Bishop John Hughes if he would officially open the event. Seán was rather wary of approaching him, as he had a reputation for being forthright and outspoken. However, he need not have worried for the Tyrone-born bishop was generous in his praise of this latest method of raising funds for the Famine victims .

'I am delighted to give my blessing to this event. A novel way of getting people together, and giving them something worthwhile to do. I am all in favour of it,' he proclaimed, his North of Ireland accent not one whit altered from when he first landed in the United States. 'A brilliant idea this, who was the genius who came up with it,' he asked.

Seán informed him that it had been the suggestion of a young girl named Mary-Anne Joyce, from Galway. The bishop asked Seán to let her know how pleased he was to participate in such a worthwhile endeavour.

'Tell me the place and the time and I will be there,' the Bishop said as Seán was leaving. 'God go with you, young man, and may He hold all you caring and charitable people in the palm of His hand henceforth. I will instruct my priests to give notice of the coming event from the pulpits from next Sunday on,' he finished.

Seán left the palace and hastened to Coburg Street to tell the Joyce family that His Lordship, Bishop Hughes would officially open the Lá Ceoil, and would also make sure that his parishioners were informed about the coming event.

'The more who knows about it, the better, isn't that so, a mhic?' Jamesy Joyce laughed, 'We need as many Irish born as is in New York and beyant to come and support the cause, and as many non-Irish as want to come along too.'

'And how are things with you, Seán,' Honor asked, as she busied herself cooking the supper.

'No complaints, thank God,' Seán answered.

'Doesn't the like of this concert comin' up put great heart into the people,' Jamesy said as they sat down to their meal, 'I'm looking forward to the music and the dancin,' it'll be like the old days'.

'True for you, Mr Joyce,' Seán agreed. 'We'll all be the better for it, those for whom the money is raised and those who helped to raise it.'

'Everyone seems to be pulling well together,' Honor observed, 'no fallin' out, no fightin' or arguing.'

Seán laughed. 'So far so good. What we don't need now is that it will rain on the day, that'd ruin everything. If it were at home in Ireland rain could be a threat, but in this country September is a good time, I believe, for an outdoor event like this.'

'Aye, that's true,' Jamesy agreed. 'When I think of all the wettins I got in the Irish summers back home! That's one of the good things about this country, when its winter its wintry, and when its summer, it is really sunny and warm.' He looked at Seán, 'Isn't that a fact?'

'This has been my first taste of an American summer,' Seán said 'and I can't dispute what you say. Little or no rain and plenty of sun, too much at times, indeed.'

'Ah, shure it is a great country, no matter what,' Jamesy puffed happily at his pipe. 'My heart's at home in Ireland, always will be, but I can see the good side of this place too, and it'll do for my time anyway.'

# Twelve

September 7th dawned a beautiful clear sunny day. In the house in Gramercy Avenue, Mary-Anne was up and about early. She wished to get her various chores carried out quickly and have her breakfast over before any of the other residents had awakened. She was filled with a tremendous excitement and anxious to be on her way to the park for the opening ceremonies which were due to begin at ten o'clock.

When she tapped on Miss Janine's bedroom door to see if she was ready for her morning bath, that young lady bade her enter and on going in Mary-Anne found her young mistress dressed and partaking of breakfast already.

'A surprise for you, dear Mary-Anne,' she declared. 'I know how busy you have been preparing for this great festival, so I decided that I would bath myself and prepare my own breakfast, so, now, dear Mary-Anne, you can run along and get yourself together for your big day.'

Mary-Anne was pleasantly surprised and said so to her young mistress.

'You are very welcome, a little surprise now and again is good for a body,' Miss Janine laughed. 'My dear grandmother is fond of quoting this to anyone who wishes to listen to her'.

Mary-Anne thanked her and returned to her own room to dress for her visit to the cathedral and the opening ceremonies.

The dead heat of August had passed and people were feeling more energetic in themselves. The early morning Mass in the cathedral had been designated an all-Irish Mass and the building was crowded. Entire families in their Sunday best filled the seats, many of them carrying baskets and rugs. When Bishop Hughes gave his homily from the altar he spoke of the unique day this was: 'Today is Lá Ceoil agus Taispeántais Ceardaíochta, the first of its kind to be held in this city. There is a great outpouring of love and concern for those at home in Ireland who are suffering such hardship, from those of us who live in fair comfort here in this great land,' he said. 'This is your opportunity to open your hearts and your purses, and it is also your chance to partake in our traditional music, crafts and games. God go with you all and may this be a day to be remembered for generations to come.'

Mary-Anne, Seán and the other members of the organising committees took their places in the large tent set up inside the entrance to the park. Behind them, pinned to the canvas, was a large map depicting the location of each stall, booth and platform area throughout the large field. There was also a free small-scale map to be given to each person as they paid their entrance fee. It was one of Mary-Anne's jobs to hand out these leaflets.

The past few weeks had been very busy, so much organising, and arranging, and long hours spent interviewing those anxious to take part in the festival. Various sections of the field had to be roped off to facilitate the events taking place there. Booths and stalls were set up for the displaying of the arts and crafts, and platforms erected for the musicians and dancers. Chairs were collected from the various church halls throughout the parishes and had to be set out. Men and women had been given posts of responsibility for the different exhibitions. The entire operation had been overseen by a group of people co-opted from the many Irish clubs and gathering places throughout the city and its environs. All help had been given on a voluntary basis. Everyone had worked well together and a great camaraderie pervaded through the weeks spent organising the festival.

The various Churches throughout New York and its surrounding areas had been asked to mention from their pulpits about this great gathering of the Irish which was taking place to collect money to be sent back to Ireland for the relief of its starving people. The priests exhorted their congregations to go along in their thousands to the park on September 7th, and to play their parts, be it through submitting craft work, helping out, or buying the produce on sale. The Irish and Irish-American newspapers were generous in advertising the event and declared that there would be no charge for this service. Newspapers from as far away as Boston and Hartford, and other major cities, took up the story of the festival and gave excellent coverage also. The new York Police Band would lead the parade from the cathedral to the park for the official opening, which would be attended by people of renown, such as the mayor, civic dignitaries, Chief of Police, and various well-known people in the New York business world. This was scheduled to take place at ten o'clock.

Mary-Anne was so anxious that everything would go according to plan that she clasped and unclasped her hands as she waited for the Lá Ceoil to begin. She was quite tired as her work schedule had been a tough one, and she had spent many a long hour helping to get everything underway. She was really amazed at the enthusiasm of the people. This coming event had unlocked the hearts and minds of many of the Irish who lived within their ghettos and who were not interested in integrating into the communities around them. The life and vitality they showed while helping and collaborating in the preparations was wonderful to witness.

"Tis a great chance to meet my own people,' one woman had told Mary-Anne, 'it'll be like home from home for us for a day.'

The same woman had proudly shown Mary-Anne the most beautiful lace work, her contribution to the craft stall. 'My mother and her mother before her were gifted with their hands. I like to do a bit meself, and my own daughters are learnin' to do this sort of work as well,' she said happily.

Other women brought their lovely handiwork for inspection. All enjoyed this opportunity to show off what they could do and there was a brightness in their eyes and a spring in their step which had been missing for a long time. The men too, had worked hard to produce items for the various booths, such as woodcarvings, pampooties, criosanna, súgán stools, chairs and leatherwork. All these items had to be priced and displayed to their best advantage.

In the distance the sound of music began to filter through to the park and a quiver of excitement went through the people already assembled. A great gathering of people followed the band as they entered the gateway. Resplendent in their uniforms, the men of the New York Police Department marched proudly along, their instruments glinting in the sunlight. Mary-Anne and Seán stood together and watched the people as they came through into the field. The entry fee was a very reasonable one, but there would be a fair enough sum gathered judging by the crowd.

There was a roll of drums heralding the arrival of the open carriage with Bishop John Hughes, and he happily acknowledged the clamorous welcome he received by raising his hands in blessing over the gathering. He left his carriage and mounted the dais to officially open the Day of Music and Craft, 'Lá Ceoil agus Taispeántais Ceardaíochta'. His speech was brief, but warm and enthusiastic as he declared the day officially open. He finished by saying in ringing tones 'Éire beo, Éire go deo'. This was greeted with loud and prolonged applause.

The booths and stalls were opened for business and the display of home crafts and 'cottage industries' was magnificent.

People strolled around in the bright sunshine, stopping at the stalls to look and to purchase. The lacework booth had an audience on a continual basis. Several women were giving demonstrations on the art of lacemaking. The onlookers were enthralled as they watched the pattern for the lacework being pricked onto parchment with a needle which was fitted with a bobbin, and pins were then used to follow the pattern. Whitework was also demonstrated to the attentive audience. This was done by cutting through the layers of paper pattern, muslin and machine net. When the sewing was completed the pattern was then torn away and the muslin cut to reveal a delicate sprinkling of flowers or other design on the net. Hand spinning was also demonstrated, as was crios making, a craft which originated on the Aran Islands. Appliqué patchwork and quilting was explained to the watching people. Aunt Bina was working a spinning wheel. She admitted to Mary-Anne that she was charmed to have been asked to do a demonstration on it. Since Honor was in charge of this particular stall, she had roped in many of her friends and acquaintances, who were experts at various crafts, to help out.

In a corner stall a cobbler had set up his stand to demonstrate his bootmaking prowess. There was a crowd around him and his skill with the last, awl and wax-end was closely watched and the finished products were passed from hand to hand for inspection. At another stand a group of young girls were busily engaged in weaving St Brigid crosses and corn knots from rushes brought from upstate in New York for this purpose. Mary-Anne had herself woven St Brigid crosses at home in Galway, even though this craft was more relevant to the Kildare area.

Mary-Anne and Seán left the main gate and walked around the field watching with great pleasure the busy stalls - no shortage of customers, it would seem. The home-baked cakes and biscuits were already sold out and the women in charge were engaged in counting the money taken in. It had been agreed at the final committee meeting that Seán Thornton would be in charge of the financial end of the festival. Each stall holder had been instructed to hand in their accounts and cash to him in the main tent, when their business was completed. He stopped at the cake stall to sort out their money situation, and Mary-Anne continued on until she came to her dad and Uncle Arthur's section. They had their travelling forge set up, the anvil, portable forge, and their toolbox in place. A horse was patiently chewing oats in his nosebag as the men gave a demonstration of the art of shoeing a horse. The acrid stench and the sizzle of the red hot iron shoes as they were plunged into the cooling water was very familiar to Mary-Anne, as she had taken lunch to the two men at their forge in the city many times. She stayed with them and chatted about the turn-out and the amount of money which would hopefully be taken in.

At twelve o'clock the musicians, singers, and dancers began to take their places on the platforms. The fiddlers plied their bows, the wind whistles and concertinas were tuned up, and with great vim and vigour the music began. Impromptu 'sets' started as people got the feel of the music, handclaps and cheers greeting their displays. When the musicians stopped for a 'sos beag' shouts of 'arís, arís' from the picnicking crowds encouraged them to begin afresh.

On her tour around Mary-Anne espied Tim O'Connor. He was sitting on a stool outside a small tent. In his role of 'seanchaí' he wore a white cáibín and puffed on a dúidín, and he was narrating scéals 'as Gaeilge' to an attentive audience. He really looks the part, Mary-Anne smiled to herself, and he is healthy again, thanks be to God.

'Mary-Anne, Mary-Anne,' called an excited voice. Miss Janine, wearing a yellow-sprigged muslin dress and carrying a matching parasol was standing with her parents at the tea tent. Mary-Anne hurried towards them; they were carrying various sized packages, and looked quite happy and contented.

'Good morning, Mary-Anne,' Mrs Wiseman smiled. 'This is a wonderful occasion, you must be very pleased with how well everything is going along.'

'Good moning, Madam, Sir, and Miss Janine,' Mary-Anne said happily, 'Yes, it has turned out even better than we hoped.'

'We have been buying some of the lovely craft work, the lace and the crochet and other lovely things,' Miss Janine said. 'Mama purchased a magnificent lace collar and sleeve trims for Grandmama, also, and look what I bought, Mary-Anne,' she opened her basket and produced a corn knot, beautifully woven.

'Yes, it is lovely work, isn't it,' agreed Mary-Anne.

'I will keep it forever,' Miss Janine said, 'in memory of this lovely day,' and she rewrapped the little corn knot and put it carefully back into her basket.

# Thirteen

Mary-Anne excused herself from the Wiseman family and was turning away to continue on her walk around the field when Mrs Wiseman suggested that perhaps Miss Janine might accompany her.

'Doctor and I will rest ourselves for a short while in the refreshment tent, you young ladies have plenty of energy,' she said to the two girls. 'Run along now and enjoy the day.'

Miss Janine was quite agreeable to walk around the park and view the proceedings. The sun was shining, it was not too warm, and she was quite interested in the various activities being carried on. When they neared Tim O'Connor's 'seanchaí' tent, Mary-Anne asked her if she wanted to listen in to his story-telling.

'Oh, yes indeed, that would be fun,' she said. 'I trust he is quite better now, Mary-Anne?'

'Yes, thank God, he appears to be back to full health,' Mary-Anne said, 'I have not had much opportunity to meet or speak with him since he came out of the hospital. I have had but little spare time this past while.'

'We will sit and listen to his stories so,' Miss Janine decreed. The two girls seated themselves on chairs on the outer edge of the audience. Tim had not seen them as yet, so they were able to watch him unobserved. He was speaking 'as Gaeilge', and his listeners were obviously enjoying what he was relating to them, if their laughter was anything to go by. Poor Miss Janine was lost between the Gaelic language and Tim's exaggerated accent, and really had no idea what was going on. She was, however, quite content to sit and watch her 'hero' which, as she had confided to Mary-Anne, was how she now regarded Tim. She had accompanied Mary-Anne to visit him on a couple of occasions, and as Tim's health gradually improved, he would walk with them in the grounds of the hospital and the three of them would converse happily together.

There was rousing applause when the 'seanchaí' finally came to the end of his rambling scéal. He informed his listeners that as his throat was dry he was going to take a 'sos beag', and get himself a cool drink. Mary-Anne and Miss Janine remained in their seats and as the crowd began to drift away Tim saw them, and discarding his cáibín and snuffing out his dúidín, came across to join them.

'Well, have you ladies ever heard a better shenachi in your entire lives,' he wanted to know.

The two girls laughed and Miss Janine admitted that she had not understood one word of what he had been saying.

'Shure and how could you,' Tim said, 'You'll have to take lessons in the Irish language, Miss.'

Miss Janine smiled and said boldly, 'Would you be willing to teach the Irish to me?' Then realising what she had said, she blushed and hung her head.

Tim gave Mary-Anne a wink, and said, looking at the downcast head: 'Nothing would give me greater pleasure than to teach this beautiful language to Miss Janine Wiseman.'

Mary-Anne hid a smile. Tim and Miss Janine had become very good friends since the fire and he would tease her as he would Mary-Anne.

Miss Janine raised her head and looked searchingly at Tim.

'Do you really mean that, Tim' she asked.

Tim did not hesitate. 'If you are serious about wanting to learn something of the Irish language, then certainly I will teach you and be glad to do so,' he smiled at her. 'It isn't an easy language to understand. My own Irish is fireside Irish, I grew up knowing it, but, I'll do my best for you.'

'Oh, yes, Tim, I am very serious about this,' Miss Janine insisted. 'I hope to visit Ireland sometime, and to have a knowledge of the language would be of great benefit, would it not?'

'Aye, that's true,' Tim agreed. He turned to Mary-Anne and asked, 'How are you, Mary-Anne, isn't this a great turn-out altogether?' He gestured around the field, 'There will be a fair deal of money to be sent to Ireland after today.'

'We hope so,' Mary-Anne said. 'So far everything is going well, and the crowd is even more than we bargained for, some of the stalls are sold out already.'

The three of them turned towards the refreshment tent, and went into its cool interior. There were many people sitting at the tables, drinking tea or coffee, and there was a buzz of conversation. Seán Thornton was seated with Pat Kennedy and another man close by the entrance flap. When he espied his three friends he come over and asked them to join him. He introduced the third person as Thomas D'Arcy Magee, the editor of the *Boston Pilot*, who on hearing of the plan for the great outdoor fleadh, had come down from Boston to see for himself this great gathering of the Irish.

They spoke together about life in the great city compared with life at home in rural Ireland, and the adjusting that had to be done by those unfamiliar with it. Mr D'Arcy Magee spoke to them about how life was for the Irish emigrants in in Boston. He said that the first Census of Boston in 1845 showed the alarmingly high number of Irish in the city and the effect of this on the housing situation. Many of these people were forced to live in appalling conditions. He told them that in actual fact Boston was not suited to take in large numbers of emigrants. If a person wanted to leave the city they had to pay tolls to cross the bridges. This meant that the poverty-stricken immigrants within the city were forced to stay there. The Irish crowded together in space which was utterly and totally inadequate. The gardens of houses were covered in shanties, rooms were divided and sub-divided. A dollar and a half was charged for each room, and if the rent wasn't paid the unfortunate tenant was instantly evicted. He himself had visited one area where in one room there were ten people, living, eating, sleeping and drinking. There were even businesses being carried on in the same houses, where goods like fruit and vegetables were sold - a serious danger to the health of the customers. There was even drink, or 'grog' as it was most commonly called, sold as well, which didn't benefit the people when disease was rampant. The first outbreak of cholera in Boston had been discovered a couple of months previously and the first person to die of this dreaded disease was an Irishman. People were living in such crowded conditions that self respect was no longer possible and disorder and intemperance reigned throughout the shanty towns. In many cases, he continued, entire families, father, mother, sons and daughters slept together in the one bed. High hopes and noble virtues cannot withstand this type of living for very long. Despair and degradation gradually took over and people just gave up and merely existed.

Seán and Pat and the two girls were fascinated listening to this man who, evidently, had considerable experience of his subject. When he asked his audience if they were bored by his conversation, they begged him to continue.

These poor people, he went on, had left one of the most beautiful countries in the entire world. To have to leave the rugged and wild charms of West Cork and Kerry, the rich plains of Meath and Kildare, the purple mountains and the lovely bay of Galway, the craggy rocks and wonderful scenery of Donegal, to live in emigrant slums in a foreign country, sure it had to have a severe psychological effect on them. As a result of this, people drowned their sorrows in the cheap liquor, or 'grog' as it was commonly called, which was brewed in these shanty areas. Fighting and drunkenness became the hallmark of the Irish in Boston. Last year, for example, most of the people taken in by the law for misdemeanours and attempts to murder, were Irish.

Pat Kennedy interposed, 'Isn't it true that New York is a far tougher and more violent city than Boston?'

'Yes, that is true,' Mr D'Arcy Magee agreed, 'but, it

is also a very wealthy city, with fine houses, concert rooms, play houses and much evidence of money.'

'Of course, there are many things need changing in this fine city,' Seán said, 'such as pigs roaming at will through the streets. The first occasion on which I witnessed this I could not believe my eyes. The pigs were wandering around, snuffling and rooting out garbage, attacking small children and leaving dirt and filth everywhere.'

'I have heard that cattle have on occasion got on to the streets also,' Pat Kennedy said, 'and the problem of stray dogs, particularly when the weather is hot and sultry, is a major one. Do you know that I encountered one such dog only last week. He was crawling along the street, foaming at the mouth. Luckily one of the city dog-killers came along and clubbed him to death.'

Mary-Anne uttered a cry of protest. 'Oh, how awful, the poor creature.'

'Not in this case, young lady,' Mr D'Arcy Magee spoke, 'to be bitten by one of these rabid dogs could result in contracting rabies, a dreadful disease, horrendous and incurable.'

'Talking about the fine streets of New York,' Seán said, 'it is a shame that these great thoroughfares are mere dirt tracks in places, the surfaces deeply holed, and at times to travel over them in a horse carriage is a precarious undertaking. Many a fine carriage has lost a wheel, or a fine carriage horse damaged a leg on these streets.'

'The City Inspector has the entire weight of the problems of this city on his shoulders,' Tim O'Connor remarked. 'The poor man hasn't a hope of getting a proper job done, there are so many trades in operation in the city, such as slaughter houses, bone boiling, and glue making. The stench at times is appalling, but money is being made by some, and it is a safe bet that the people who make the money from these filthy trades, do not live in the vicinity where it is made.'

Mary-Anne and Miss Janine were fascinated listening to the men conversing on these things. Neither of them had any input to make as the area in which they lived was well away from the stench filled and filth covered section being mentioned. James and Honor were blessed in the accommodation in which they lived, Bina and Arthur had made sure that they would be provided with the best they could find having plenty of experience themselves of inadequate and 'emigrant barracks' type housing.

Mr D'Arcy Magee ventured his opinion that 'it has been a very strange accident that a people who, in Ireland, hungered and thirsted for land, who struggled for conacre and cabin, even to the shedding of blood, when they reached the New World, in which a day's wages would have purchased an acre of wild land in fee, wilfully concurred to sink into the condition of a miserable town tenantry, to whose squalor, even European seaports would hardly present a parallel'.

'We are a contrary race, it must be said,' Seán said.

'Indeed yes.' agreed D'Arcy Magee, 'the Irish are getting a bad name, and are slowly but surely sinking into a morass of despair. There is no way out of the poverty trap for most, if not all, of these people. They left their own land to escape death from hunger, but are now having to deal with another form of "death", the death of hope, ideals and the expectation of a glorious future in the great land of America.'

Tim ventured to say, 'But, it is a fact that we Irish have survived against the most extraordinary odds, unjust wars, Cromwell, famine ... '

D'Arcy Magee agreed with him and said, 'We will survive in Boston and in New York, and other major cities too, and in future years great families will spring up from these survivors, and will make their mark in the world'.

When Mr Magee had finished speaking, there was a brief silence as the five young people considered what he had been saying, and then Pat Kennedy spoke: 'I am strongly tempted to travel to Boston myself. It's a place I would like to visit, even though, having listened to you, sir, it does not appear to be a wholesome one. I am a strong man from a health point of view, and I have my trade as a bricklayer. Boston will have to build to house these people properly, and I mean to be there when that starts to happen.'

'Look me up when you arrive in the city, young man,' D'Arcy Magee told him. 'We need young, healthy and go ahead people like yourself; I'll give you whatever help I can to get you started.'

# Fourteen

When D'Arcy Magee had made his farewells, the five young people remained at the table. They had found his topic of conversation an enthralling one, but also a depressing one. It would seem that very few of the Irish who had fled from Ireland and the unjust treatment they received there would ever make their mark on the social or political life of the cities in which they now lived. Tim considered that it would take the life span of two or three generations before the natural Irish intelligence, wit and quickness of understanding would assert themselves, and the descendants of the poor immigrants, 'such as we are ourselves,' would become powerful and successful in years ahead.

'We will not be around to witness this,' he continued, 'would to God that we could, I'd be a proud man then.'

'We Irish are a great race of people. We have never been entirely crushed,' Seán asserted, 'even though many have tried to do just that. There is always a little spark left in some corner of our understanding, which can be rekindled and encouraged to flame. Rebellions have occurred in every century, some successful, some fiascos. It is in the very nature of us Irish to withstand that which is unjust and ill meant, and come out fighting,' he finished, and laughed when Pat Kennedy clapped his hands in appreciation.

"Tis true for you, Seán, you can never keep good

men down.'

The three men began to reminisce about life in Ireland in their time. The terrible conditions prevailing, towns and villages with no sanitation, where drainage was unknown. People never bothered to wash themselves or their clothes. After months of starvation there was not the strength to haul water from the nearest river or lake, and there was no money to buy fuel to heat the water, even if it was procured. The same conditions prevailed in the cities in which they were now living in America. Apathy and inertia pervaded their lives even here. People huddled together in the cold winters in New York too, very often joined by passers-by, and neighbours. No one was ever turned away, and all slept huddled together to keep warm.

'Some things never change,' commented Pat Kennedy, 'disease is passed on in these conditions, lice infected people pass on the disease of typhus, and other dreadful afflictions.'

Mary-Anne was feeling uncomfortable during this conversation; it was bringing back memories which she had pushed to the back of her mind. She always felt angry and helpless at how little she could do for the people at home. Her great hope now was that the festival would be a success, and that money would be sent to Ireland to help even in a small way. Miss Janine had had very little to say, and Mary-Anne noticed that she paled somewhat when the word 'typhus' was mentioned, and when Seán mentioned the dirt and filth in which people were forced to live because no money had been invested in proper sanitation and drainage, she gave a little cry of protest.

This recalled the men to the business of the day and they made haste to return to their various posts outside in the field. Tim put on his cáibín and lit up his dúidín preparatory to returning to his seanchaí spot, and the two girls wended their way towards the craft and food corner of the field. The crowd were good humoured and the singing and music continued unabated. No one seemed to want to go home at all, and families were still sitting around on the grass enjoying the sunshine and the enterainment being provided for them.

Seán and Pat went to the tent at the entrance gate and at Seán's insistence, Pat took up a position at the opening flap to oversee the boxes of money as they were handed in for checking.

Despite what he had said to reassure Mary-Anne after she had been accosted by the two men, Seán had taken this happening very seriously. He had confided to some of the committee members his fears that an attack of some kind was likely to be made on him or on the proceeds of the festival, and consquently several men had been on guard duty throughout the day.

Seán had confided to Tim his worry about possible trouble at the festival, particularly when the cash had been collected and counted, before being taken to the Bank. Tim had suggested that an arrangement could be made for an armed policeman, in mufti, to be in the tent throughout the day. The knowledge of this arrangement would be known only to Seán and himself. 'The less who know about this, the better,' he said, 'where loaded guns are involved innocent people could be hurt and we do not want that.'

Seán had protested that even one armed policeman might be overdoing the security bit, but Tim assured him that 'America isn't Ireland, the gun is a big deterrent here, believe me'. Seán agreed to go along with this plan, 'with the help of God there'll be no need for the gun to be produced at all,' he said.

The boxes brought in were being emptied and counted on tables set at the rear of the tent. The men on guard duty stood close to the cashiers. The armed police officer maintained his position close to the entrance flap. His ostensible function throughout the day was to hand out tickets for the refreshment tent and the map giving the details of the location of the different stalls and sideshows throughout the field. Since he was a friend of Tim, who had 'volunteered' to assist on the day, none of the committee members questioned his presence.

Seán's worry that there could be an attack of some kind levelled at the festival was apparently unfounded as the day was now drawing to a close and no problem had arisen. He breathed a sigh of relief and sat down to help in the reckoning of the cash already handed in by some of the stall holders.

# Fifteen

The biggest event of the day was due to start at 3.30 in the afternoon. This was the 'Potato Pickin'' competition. Since the Lá Ceoil was being staged primarily for the raising of funds for famine victims in Ireland in which the loss of the potato played a major part, it had been suggested that a special event, incorporating the potato would be held. This idea was the brainchild of Bina and Arthur, along with several of their friends, who were well known in the business life of New York city, and who had also agreed to make large donations so as to be able to participate in this special event.

The plan was thus: ten rows of potatoes, each fifty yards long, would be laid down: at a given signal, selected persons of renown in the city, such as the Chief Fire Officer, the Chief of Police, city councillors, business and trade Executives, shop and department store owners, and others of high standing in the commercial life of the city, would endeavour, while running down these lines, to fill a pail with the potatoes. At the end of each run there was a large weighing machine where each pail of potatoes would be weighed and recorded. The 'run' would continue until all athe potatoes had been gathered and weighed. Whoever had picked the heaviest weight of potatoes would be awarded a 'potato pickin'' plaque at a special ceremony in the evening. This would be presented by Bishop John Hughes at a function in the large tent. Festival day would then officially be at an end.

Bets would be taken by 'bookmakers' as to who would have the greatest weight of 'potatoes' when the 'run' ended. All proceeds would, of course, go towards the Famine fund.

Since this event was a new one, great interest had been shown by all the participants. There would be considerable advertising value attached to it, as the newspapers were anxious to give it good coverage.

Standing on a platform and using a police megaphone, Richard Gorman, one of the organisers of the committee, announced to the large crowd that the day's entertainment was drawing to a close. The 'Potato Pickin' competition was now scheduled to take place, and if the contestants would take their places it could be got underway. The potato lines were already laid out and bets could be put down from this moment. There were men on duty acting as bookmakers throughout the field.

Following this announcement there was a rush of people towards the designated area. Mothers and fathers laden down with picnic equipment and clutching small children made their way there, all talking excitedly. Older men and women, anxious to secure good vantage positions, hurried along, laughing and calling out to the competitors, 'Our good money is on ye, don't let us down'.

The competitors lined up, their numbers pinned to their chests and backs, their pails in their hands, some looking anxious, others, as befitted their stations in life, appeared unconcerned. That they had faced more difficult tasks in their public lives than 'pickin' potatoes' was the impression they conveyed. Mary-Anne and Miss Janine were quite close to the potato lines and were able to get a clear view of the competitors. To their delight they espied Dr Wiseman, pail in hand, taking up his position in the line-out. He was looking somewhat selfconscious, but determined to do his best.

'Papa, Papa,' called Miss Janine, 'Run fast for us.' He looked in their direction and gave them a quick smile. The starting bell clanged and the 'potato pickin'' competition got underway.

Some of the competitors took off at a great rate, grabbing at the potatoes, missing some, getting others. The more rotund found bending down a bit difficult and consequently had to make several attempts before succeeding in getting one or two potatoes into their pails. One or two tripped themselves up in their eagerness, and the potatoes they had already collected rolled out of the pail and scattered all over the field. These had to be retrieved and this meant that the pickers had to cut across the lanes of the other competitors. Several people landed on the ground in a laughing tangle, and as a consequence, more pails overturned and their contents scattered all over the place. The crowd roared their encouragement, screaming and laughing at the mix up. The bell sounded and the pails were then weighed and noted and the collectors sent back to the starting line again. The signal was given and the 'potato pickers' galloped along the lines, bending to pick and put whatever they could grab into their pails. Their audience continued to yell and scream encouragement, many of them laughing so much that the tears ran down their faces. To see the 'pillars of society' of the city of New York in such undignified positions as they scrambled and fought over the humble 'prátaí' was absolutely hilarious to watch.

Dr Wiseman, who had hitched up the legs of his trousers for ease in running, had lost his hat somewhere along the way. With determination written all over him, he bent and picked, bent and picked at a great rate.

'Hurry, Papa, hurry,' Miss Janine shouted at him, 'you are winning, you are winning.' Her bonnet was askew, and her ringlets tumbled about her face, as she ran along the sideline encouraging her father. Mrs Wiseman had gathered her skirts, and discarded her shoes so that she could keep pace with the competitors. Mary-Anne was delighted as she watched staid people forgetting their dignity and whooping and hollering as good as the rest of the by now, close to hysterical audience.

The final bell clanged when the last potato had been picked and pailed, and the anxious competitors lined up for the weighing-in ceremony and for the announcment of the winner. The Chief Fire Officer had weighed in more potatoes than any of the other contestants, and was therefore declared the winner. Dr Wiseman was selected as first runner-up. Anyone would have believed that he had in fact come first the way his wife and daughter hugged and kissed him. He looked very pleased with himself and acknowledged the applause of the crowd with a smile and a bow.

The Chief Fire Officer was congratulated by the chairman of the organising commitee, and the crowd roared their approval of his win. The other 'pickers' were called up one by one, and they acknowledged the approbation of the crowd with pleased smiles.

There was no doubt that the 'potato pickin'' competition was a fitting finale act for the Lá Ceoil. There was a good deal of good-natured chat as their audience made their way out of the park. 'We'll have to do this every year,' 'It was a wonderful day altogether,' 'It was like being at home for the day,' were some of the comments overheard by the committee members on gate duty. These remarks were joyfully reported to the organisers at an impromptu meeting held in the refreshment tent later.

# Sixteen

His Lordship, Bishop John Hughes had a special word for Mary-Anne when she was introduced to him at the presentation ceremony. He congratulated her on the 'Lá Ceoil agus Taispeántais Ceardaíochta'. 'A brilliant idea,' he said, and remarked that he was particularly pleased at the way in which the people co-operated so well.

'We have got ourselves a bad name with all the drinking and carry-on that goes along with it,' he said, 'but today, has shown that, given a chance, the Irish people will acquit themselves extremely well. It has been a proud day for me to be associated with this very well-conducted event. The cause for which it was held will benefit greatly, thanks be to the Lord, and our people here will benefit greatly, be it in a different way, as well. God bless you child.' Mary-Anne knelt to kiss his ring, and as she rose, he said to her, quietly, 'this country needs the like of you Mary-Anne, your courage and determination will not go unrewarded'.

The presentations were finally completed and Bishop Hughes made his way to his carriage. He was surrounded by well-wishers and he raised his hand in a final blessing over the crowd before his coachman clucked up the horses and he was driven away to his palace.

Mary-Anne, Seán, Pat Kennedy, Tim and Miss Janine stood together, watching the carriage until it disappeared from their view.

'Are you tired out, Mary-Anne,' Seán enquired.

'No, not at all,' Mary-Anne smiled at him. 'Everything went so well that I am not a bit tired, only delighted that we succeeded in having such a marvellous day for everyone.'

'The final counting of the money has to be done,' Seán said. 'We need an extra pair of hands, can you spare a little more of your time before you leave for Gramercy Avenue?'

Mary-Anne agreed to stay a little longer, and then recalled that Miss Janine had said that she was feeling a little weary, and wished to return home. Mary-Anne mentioned this to Seán and Tim, and was grateful when Tim offered to accompany that young lady to her home.

'After all, Mary-Anne,' he said, 'this is your one day entirely free from looking after Miss Janine, so stay where you are and I'll see to it that your young mistress gets home safely.' He looked across at Miss Janine, who smiled happily at him, and said 'Thank you, Tim, I would not wish Mary-Anne to have to leave here before this great day is finally over'.

Tim wished Mary-Anne, Seán and Pat the best of luck in 'the counting house' as he put it, and offering his arm to Miss Janine the two of them went away in the direction of the main gateway where the hansom cabs were lined up awaiting possible custom following the ending of the Lá Ceoil.

Seán, Mary-Anne and Pat went back inside the tent and resumed the checking and totalling of the cash boxes. Dick O'Connell and James Morgan were working away as well. Mary-Anne had revised her opinion of these two men, as she had worked closely with them for some weeks now: it was their associates whom she distrusted and feared.

When the final total was announced there was a concerted gasp of delight - over $1,000 in actual cash had been taken in on the day, and more money due from advertising had to be collected and then added to the day's takings. The people in the tent cheered and clapped each other on the back. A great sense of happiness pervaded, the pleasure which comes from a job well done.

'We will relieve you of that money,' a harsh voice suddenly broke in on the celebrations. To the horror and dismay of everyone in the tent, two men, brandishing guns, had entered the tent. They were masked and their attitude was cold and menacing. Mary-Anne felt Seán tense beside her, and she thought, Oh, dear God, this cannot be happening, all our hard work, the money we got for Ireland, they'll take it all away from us.

One of the men, holding his gun threateningly, stood with his back to the entrance flap, while the other man came forward and grabbed the canvas bag containing the money. As he backed away, Richard O'Connell made an involuntary movement, and in the split second that the robber glanced in his direction, Seán Thornton lashed out, catching him a hard blow to the back and knocking him off balance. At the same time, a scuffle broke out to the rear, and a voice with a strong Kerry accent was heard exclaiming 'Did ye think we'd let ye get away with it, eh? Drop that gun, I tell you, drop it'.

Tim O'Connor had a firm grip on the masked man

at the entrance, and the man, who had earlier in the day helped Mary-Anne to hand out the guide maps, snapped handcuffs on the man Seán was holding.

It had all happened so fast, the attempted robbery, the guns pointed at them, Seán attacking the masked man, and then, Tim O'Connor, who was supposed to be escorting Miss Janine - where had he come from? Mary-Anne shook her head in bewilderment.

'It's all right, Mary-Anne,' Seán Thornton came over to where she was standing, 'everything is all right now.'

'Oh, Seán, I thought that all our lovely money was gone,' Mary-Anne cried. 'Those awful men, and you, you could have been killed.'

'We figured out that something like this could happen,' Seán explained 'and so we were well prepared.'

'But, Tim, where did Tim come from, I thought he was taking Miss Janine back to Gramercy Avenue,' Mary-Anne asked.

'Miss Janine wishing to go home was the ideal way for Tim to be outside of here. She is quite safe over in the refreshment tent with her parents,' Seán explained. 'We had to behave as normally as possible. Tim, being a police officer, had a strategy worked out in the event of an attempted robbery, and, thank the Lord, the plan worked out well.'

'Seán, I just can't grasp what happened,' Mary-Anne was still bewildered. 'You took a chance, you could have been killed.' She reached out and laid her hand on his arm.

'Well, I wasn't, I'm here, safe and sound,' Seán laughed down at her. 'We couldn't let anyone steal all our hard earned money, could we now, Mary-Anne?'

'No, we couldn't,' Mary-Anne had to laugh too, 'and Seán, I'm so glad that you were here with me when all this happened.'

'Are you, Mary-Anne, are you truly glad that I was here with you?' Seán's face was suddenly serious.

Mary-Anne looked at him. She studied the face of the young man who meant everything in the world to her, his steady blue eyes, which were now looking at her very seriously.

This is an important moment in my life, she thought, God help me to say the right thing.

'Yes, Seán,' she smiled shyly at him. 'I am always glad when you are with me, even in the middle of an armed robbery.' She gave a little nervous laugh, and then gasped as Seán put his arms around her, and bending down kissed her on the lips, gently and tenderly. Then he said quietly 'Is tú grá mo chroí, Máire Aine. I'll always want to be with you, forever and ever, but, only if that is what you wish too'.

Mary-Anne, who had never been kissed by anyone other than members of her family, was rosy red with shyness, looked around her, but, apparently no one else in the tent was taking any notice of Seán and herself. She placed her two hands on his shoulders and looking up at him, smiled and said: 'Yes, Seán, that is what I wish, that you will always be with me, forever and ever more.'

# Seventeen

Tim O'Connor held the letter which had been handed to him by the sister in charge of the ward where Thomas Hayden had died early that morning.

'We found this letter in his pocket, addressed to his family in Ireland. Perhaps you will see that they get it.' The sister looked sad, 'We hoped that he might pull through, but it was not to be.'

Tim, deeply grieved by the death of his friend, said 'I will look after it, I'll make sure that his family get it'.

Leaving the hospital Tim put the letter carefully in his pocket. Thomas Hayden would be buried in the cemetery attached to the hospital, following a funeral Mass being held on the morrow. A brave young man, his funeral costs would be paid by the money donated by the men of the precinct to which he was attached. Any surplus would be forwarded to his family in Ireland. Tim agreed to look after this and was now returning to his lodging house to write to the Hayden family and give them the sad news.

Tim was going back to Ireland within the next two weeks. Following the attempted robbery after the end of the Lá Ceoil, it was agreed, at a special meeting of the committee, that the money collected at that event, should be taken to Ireland by a trustworthy person. Tim had been chosen and had joyfully accepted their decision. His superior officers had sanctioned his leave of absence for several months, and to crown his delight, he had received top marks in his recent final law examination. He would be meeting his family again for the first time in over five years, and would be able to see for himself just how things were with them.

Mary-Anne was delighted for him, she knew just how much he wished to return to Ireland to see his family.

'Say hello to Ireland for me, won't you Tim,' she said to him, 'I know that I will be going back myself as soon as I can, but in the meantime kiss the ground for me when you step onto it, until I can do it for myself.'

Tim said that he surely would do that for her. He was glad that Mary-Anne was so happy now, and in his heart he knew that Seán Thornton was the right man for her. However, she would always be his own dear friend, and he would be hers.

Miss Janine was upset that Tim was leaving for Ireland, but brightened up somewhat when she realised that Ireland was but a short trip away when she visited England on her European travels.

'Perhaps I will visit Ireland and County Kerry,' she said to Tim when the four friends had visited 'Frau Gruber's for a meal following an outing together.

'You do that, Miss Janine,' Tim agreed, 'My mam and dad will give you a right royal welcome, and I'll show you around my beautiful County of Kerry and further afield.'

The four of them walked along companionably. Miss Janine had her hand tucked inside the arm of Tim O'Connor, while Mary-Anne and Seán were holding hands. It being the fall of the year, the leaves on the trees were turning to russet and gold along the wide thoroughfare of Fifth Avenue. The air was clear and fresh, the skies blue and unclouded.

A good time of the year before the onset of winter and then a new year. A good time to be alive for Mary-Anne, Seán, Tim and Miss Janine.

# Eighteen

Three thousand miles away, across the Atlantic ocean, in Ireland, the lives of the people, which had been dismal and grey for many years, were brightened by the impending arrival in the country of the young Queen Victoria. She was the first monarch to set foot in the County of Cork. Unfortunately, the harsh realities of life in the famine-torn country were not to be on display for Her Royal Highness. Since cholera was rampant throughout the land, the chosen route for her journey from County Cork to Dublin was kept a safe distance from the disease-ridden and starving people.

Prior to the arrival of the Queen there was considerable dissent among those who would be expected to make the arrangements for the royal visit. Some of them refused to participate, saying that the Queen would not be pleased by an ostentatious display of expensive decorations and unnecessary illuminations, when she surely knew that thousands of her subjects were in dire need. They declared that the suggested adornments constituted a sham and a lie, and would that the Queen should diverge from the arranged itinerary even for the length of one mile, she would discover for herself the true nature of life in Ireland at present. Another suggested that Her Royal Highness should, by right, visit some of the workhouses, particularly those in Galway, Mayo and Roscommon. Then surely she 'will understand just what is happening in this section of her kingdom'.

There were many who wished to protest at the arrival in Ireland of this young woman, Queen Victoria, to a land which was not hers to govern. Remnants of secret societies came together to put into operation a scheme that the Queen should be seized and held hostage. However, this plan came to nothing when only a few hundred volunteers turned up at the designated rendezvous. This number was deemed insufficient to deal with the vast number of British soldiers who would be available to recover Her Majesty should the attempt to abduct her succeed.

When the news of the impending visit became known it caused a great ripple of excitement. Those in favour of the visit suggested that a certain amount of employment could accrue from such an event. A special carriage was to be constructed for the royal couple. A four-wheeled vehicle, to be drawn by four horses, royal blue in colour, with the royal coat of arms emblazoned on the doors. The interior would be covered in a rich blue fabric, a mixture of silk and wool.

Newspaper reaction to the proposed visit was not so favourable. The *Freemans Journal*, remarked that 'one visit to a hut in Connacht, one view of a "cleared estate" in the south, a pencil sketch of the kind Queen Victoria was fond of executing, showing an unroofed cabin with the "miserable emaciated inhabitants cast out and perishing on the dungheap beside it" would be a better portrait of Ireland than the beauties of Killarney'.

An announcement by the Marquess of Kildare that

the Dublin Central Relief Committee had run out of funds and that there was no possible means of obtaining any more, angered the *Evening Mail*. 'The sum of two shillings and sixpence would keep a family of five for one week, and if we have funds to spare let them be spent, not on illuminations, but on Her Majesty's starving subjects.' However, the arrangements for the visit went on regardless.

Illuminating Sackville Street and other main thoroughfares, not to mention providing suitable accommodation for the royal couple, four of their children, their staff, totalling in all some thirty-six persons, caused severe headaches for the people who had to accomplish miracles with the meagre sum of money which Charles Wood, the Chancellor of the Exchequer, deemed sufficient. Buildings, long neglected, had to be given facelifts, as they were on part of the route proposed for the royal *cortège*. Grafton Street, in particular, was in such a state of decay, it was decided that the facade of the entire street should be cleaned up and bright curtains and flower arrangements be put in place for the occasion.

Over in Galway, the village of Moneen was deserted and the smell of death and decay lingered in the air. The once cosy homes of the pre-famine days were now, in many cases, roofless, and others had their doorways and windows open to the elements. Not a creature stirred around the little clocháns nestling in the foothills of the purple mountains. The once flourishing potato ridges were overgrown by vegetation, but their outlines could be discerned on the rising ground.

The schoolhouse, which had been used for a time

by the unfortunates whose homes had been tumbled by the 'battering ram,' was now partially overgrown by ivy. The childish laughter and chatter which had once rung through the building were now just a tinkle of memory in the brooding silence which pervaded the valley. The faint echo of the music which had filled the air in the far off days of happy living there, could be imagined when the breeze rustled through the chimneys and the overhanging branches of the trees.

The Mass path, overgrown and almost indiscernible, wended its way to the roofless church. No feet had trodden their way there in many a long day, and in the little churchyard, the last resting place of entire families from the Moneen and Clonmore parishes, the grass grew high over the unmarked graves. There was no one left to whisper a prayer for the repose of their souls.

Over in Dublin, the *Times* newspaper, commenting on the crowds of people who lined the gaily decorated streets, said that the 'welcome was cordial and ardent, but that many of the people looked poor and haggard'. The Queen herself wrote in her diary, 'You see more ragged and wretched people here than I ever saw anywhere else'.

The courage of the Irish people, their pride, brought them on to the streets to cheer for the 'little Queen,' who could not possibly be expected to understand that a great nation can never be completely vanquished. Éire beo, Éire go deo.

# THE BRIGHT SPARKS FAN CLUB

## WOULD YOU LIKE TO JOIN?

Would you like to receive a **FREE** bookmark and BRIGHT SPARKS friendship bracelet?

You are already halfway there. If you fill in the questionnaire on the opposite page and one other questionnaire from the back page of any of the other BRIGHT SPARKS titles and return both questionnaires to Attic Press at the address below, you automatically become a member of the BRIGHT SPARKS FAN CLUB.

If you are, like many others, a lover of the BRIGHT SPARKS fiction series and become a member of the BRIGHT SPARKS FAN CLUB, you will receive special discount offers on all new BRIGHT SPARKS books, plus a BRIGHT SPARKS bookmark and a beautiful friendship bracelet made with the BRIGHT SPARKS colours. Traditionally friendship bracelets are worn by friends until they fall off! If your friends would like to join the club, tell them to buy the books and become a member of this book lovers' club.

Please keep on reading and spread the word about our wonderful books. We look forward to hearing from you soon.

Name _____

Address _____

_____

Age _____

For a catalogue of all books in the Bright Sparks series or to order individual titles, you can post, fax, phone or E-mail us direct at:

**Attic Press**, 29 Upper Mount St, Dublin 2. Ireland.
Tel: (01) 661 6128 Fax: (01) 661 6176
E-mail: Atticirl@iol.ie

**Attic Press** hopes you enjoyed *After the Famine*. To help us improve the **Bright Sparks** series for you please answer the following questions.

1. Why did you decide to buy this book?

_____
_____
_____

2. Did you enjoy this book? Why?

_____
_____
_____

3. Where did you buy it?

_____
_____
_____

4. What do you think of the cover?

_____
_____
_____

5. Have you ever read any other books in the **BRIGHT SPARKS** series? Which one/s?

_____
_____
_____

6. Have you any comments to make on the books in the **BRIGHT SPARKS** series?

_____
_____
_____

If there is not enough space for your answers on this coupon please continue on a sheet of paper and attach it to the coupon.
Post this coupon to **Attic Press**, 29 Upper Mount Street, Dublin 2 and we'll send you a **BRIGHT SPARKS** bookmark.

Name_____Age_____
Address _____
_____Date_____

For a catalogue of all books in the Bright Sparks series or to order individual titles, you can post, fax, phone or E-mail us direct at:
**Attic Press**, 29 Upper Mount St, Dublin 2. Ireland.
Tel: (01) 661 6128 Fax: (01) 661 6176
E-mail: Atticirl@iol.ie